Totally Bound Publishing books by Sara Ohlin

Graciella
Handling the Rancher
Seducing the Dragonfly
Flirting with Forever

My Graciella
Hearts in Bloom

Rescue Me
Salvaging Love
Igniting Love
Promising Love
Embracing Love

My Graciella

HEARTS IN BLOOM

SARA OHLIN

HEARTS IN BLOOM

Dedication

To Shannin.
My life is infinitely more beautiful with you in it.
Cheers to twenty-five years of friendship!
Love you.

Chapter One

Using the brand-new keys — two silver ones on a simple ring — Gabby unlocked the gorgeous double doors and propped them open to let the soft spring breeze flow. She stood outside for a moment, observing. Afternoon in downtown Graciella, the prettier, happier version, rising from under the decades-long shroud of oppression, was such a lovely place. Now, there was a joy and a lightness to the town. Excitement and growth, coupled with that charming small-town feel, were present everywhere.

And she was here, back in its warm embrace, finally.

To say she'd missed her home was an understatement. Part of her didn't even recognize the place anymore, but, more accurately, she was the unrecognizable one. Disillusioned, changed, but determined to prosper. She would heal her soul, shove away the last few years and claw her way back to joy and independence.

Seems so much easier to imagine than to actually do. Easy didn't have anything to do with it. It was a must, and she would succeed.

No more standing on the threshold, she ordered herself and stepped inside. One wide-open empty space greeted her. She set her bag down and slowly strolled the building's length, the clip of her sandals echoing throughout the room. It looked so much better than the gutted skeleton of a few months ago. Now it was a perfect blank slate ready for her.

Gabby knelt and ran her hands over the newly finished hardwood floors, sun-warmed and light in the brightness of a sunny day. She lay on her back, stretched out her arms and legs and smiled. *I'm here. I did it!* Sun streamed in through the windows and warmed her skin, warmed her soul. She took a deep breath and let the heat strengthen and soothe the broken pieces inside her.

The old insurance office had been sitting vacant on a pretty corner in Graciella for over fifteen years, waiting for new life. She'd ogled this spot since she was a teenager dreaming of her very own salon. Today the floors were refinished, new drywall had been hung and the old windows replaced. One wall had exposed old brick she was delighted with. Everything crappy was gone, even—*especially*—the ugly foam ceiling tiles.

Above her rose high ceilings draped in soft wood planks. This space was hers, every single battle-earned inch. She might have taken a few wrong curves in life, dated a man who crushed the light inside her, but never again. Now she was more determined than ever to bring her dream to fruition.

The beautiful light flowing in through the floor-to-ceiling windows infused her with calm, with anticipation. The floor against her back felt solid, grounding her. Her mind cleared and she focused her energy on this new space, her dream salon that she'd imagined ever since she was a young girl.

White walls, white trim and white linen curtains along the windows. It needed to be clean, crisp and bright. She'd stick with simple white cabinets for each station and brown leather salon chairs. Polished and sophisticated, that was what she was aiming for. A plant or two, scattered about. *No, one plant at the front desk or a vase of fake flowers to add one stoic pop of color. No sense cluttering up the place.* Gabby leaned into the calm picture she drew in her mind.

If she were lucky, it would only be a few more weeks until she could open. Her friend Lily's construction company had rocked things so far, and the sinks, cabinets and chairs were due to arrive this week. *Lucky?* Gabby used to consider herself lucky, but opening her own salon didn't involve luck.

Only a ton of bullshit followed by sheer, hard, bleeding determination had gotten her to where she was today. *"Moment by moment,"* her new therapist had said. *"Take things however you need, at your own pace. Sometimes all we can do is go moment by moment."*

Gabby closed her eyes as if that could ward off the ugly reminders of the past few years. She was achieving her goals, albeit a few years later than she'd planned.

She couldn't think like that. What mattered was that she was back in Graciella, her home in a gentle valley on the West Coast of Oregon, nestled into the farmland and guarded by the rugged cliffs and deep blue of the Pacific Ocean, her true place.

Those were the parts of her past that she'd resurrect. *Those are the parts that will hold me together, keep me from losing myself again. My home, my foundation.* Gabriella

Flores, infinitely smarter and a bit world-weary, was back to make a name for herself. *Successful, single and fabulous.* That was her new motto. She'd wrapped it around her being like the perfect dress, pretty but deceiving, showing off her assets, allowing others to see only what she wanted while keeping the vulnerable parts of her hidden and protected.

A cloud drifted over the sun, a shadow nudging into her vision. Gabby sensed it as sure as she had the brightness of before. Then came a touch on her cheek. "Holy shit, what the—" Gabby yelled, slamming her eyes open, her heart leaping from her chest.

"Oh! She swears like you, Daddy," a bright voice from a tiny mouth echoed above her.

Two small people were bent over her body, head-to-head, gazing at her with soft brown eyes, big and wide and sparkling with a dancing hint of gold around the rim of each iris. Dark long baby lashes, full cheeks and two halos of black curls. *Identical tiny people.*

Maybe she'd fallen down the rabbit hole of some foreign universe. Her heart raced as she blinked at the light flickering between these two tiny bodies. *The sun is still here. I feel the floors against my bones.* One child put her soft chubby hand on Gabby's cheek, patting it gently. The other had taken one of her hands and linked the two together, Gabby's larger one enveloping the small warm one.

"I think she's alive," the other tiny mouth whispered.

Suddenly a man was in her space, lifting the two brown cherubs away in a swift but careful hold, setting them behind him and kneeling his body down beside Gabby. "Are you okay? Where are you hurt? Don't move." Large hands mapped her body, gently but with intention. One hand stopped at her throat. Two shaking

10

fingers felt for her pulse. He moved both hands to her chest.

"Whoa," she said, pulling his wrists away from her boobs. "Stop...stop. I'm fine."

Gray short-sleeved T-shirt, baseball hat and sunglasses were right in her face. Whoever he was, he was breathing as if he'd just scaled a mountain at a record pace to get to her. His body vibrated under her hands and his backpack pressed against her thigh. "I..."

Something was happening. He was warmer than the sun. All she was doing was holding his wrists and she wanted to run the pads of her thumbs across the sensitive skin, feel his pulse beating, concentrate on its rhythm. Gabby shut her eyes again and tried to steady her own breathing. *What's happening?* It was like —

"Christ!" he yelled and jerked upright to standing. "What are you doing?"

Gabby blinked. Something in her tugged at the loss of his touch. Confused, she raised her eyes up his body. Old running shoes and shorts, he towered above her, hands on his hips, no longer shaking, or at least she couldn't tell. Body held rigid in anger, he shoved his sunglasses off his face and glared at her. He was tall with broad shoulders blocking the sun completely now with his angry warrior silhouette, a pink cross-body bag strapped across his chest.

"Uh...thinking?" she answered. She blinked again to clear the fog in her vision. *What the hell is happening?*

"Passed out on the floor?" He crossed his arms over his chest.

Wait just a second. She lifted herself off the floor and stood to face him. She did not enjoy being yelled at, and especially not while he towered above her. "Why are you yelling at me? Who are you? I... This is mine." She pointed to the floor and the windows, stepping out of his shadow to allow the warm rays to calm her heart. She wasn't afraid, not exactly. He was acting like a jerk, but the pink bag, the cartoon characters on his shirt and the two tiny humans who belonged to him whisked away any hesitation.

Rigid and angry, there was not one single ounce of kindness on his face. Gabby crossed her own arms — she could project warrior too — and met his stare. *Scowl more like it.* Gabby sucked in a breath. Eyes the same shade as her Pacific, deep swirling blue, stared back at her. Everything safe and exciting all rolled into one color. *Home.*

No, nope, no way. She shook her head and took a step back. That can't be right. *He's not my home. He's not my foundation. I don't even know this rude man.* Weird emotions surged through her. She glanced at her surroundings and grounded herself in this new space that would soon be her salon.

This is my home. Graciella. I'm already here, in my safe place, all by myself, exactly as I want.

Chapter Two

"Look, Daddy," Emilia said from her spot on the floor. "I bet she was making sunshine angels."

Tessa joined Emi on the large sunny spot on the hardwoods and flapped her legs and arms.

"It's snow angels and you do it in winter, girls," Luca said. *Shit*, he was a complete mess. His pulse wanted to jackhammer out of his skin. He tried to relax his wrists that he'd braced tightly to stop the shaking. Sweat pooled on the back of his neck and he tried to gather what the hell he was doing, while this woman stared at him as if she'd seen a ghost, or maybe a monster.

He had practically mauled her. But she'd been passed out, *hurt, dead.* He tore his hat off and wiped his face. That old sick monster tried to surge up in him. *Beat it back, Rossi. She's not dead. She's not dead.* She was a normal person doing whatever the hell she wanted on the floor of an abandoned shop in downtown Graciella. It wasn't any of his business. *Breathe. White walls, hardwood floors, his girls on the floor. Notice what's real.*

"You can do sun angels too," Tessa insisted in her small whisper. "But it's not as comfy."

"It's sooo warm, though. I love the warm. Was that what you were doing, pretty lady, sunshiny angels?"

"I…" The woman ran her fingers along her neck, mouth half open, gazing between him and his twins. Her dark brown hair was caught in a barrette and big curls framed her face. He wanted to wrap his hand around that neck, check her pulse, feel her alive and breathing, make sure of it.

"Let's go, girls," he said, holding out his hands. He had to get out of here now before he lost more of his shit.

"But it's nice down here." Emi pouted. "You should try it, Daddy."

Maybe he should. Maybe the ground would mask the fact that he'd just revisited his past in a way that shocked his blood. But he needed to get out of the sun, not bask in it. It was a million degrees in here. "Time for ice cream — don't want to miss that, do you?"

The girls gasped and scrambled to grab his hands.

Their tiny hands… He never got tired of marveling at how busy and full of life those hands were, how much trouble they could get into, how soft they were in his and how trusting. They anchored him to solid ground. Gripping each of them, he turned and led them outside.

"Can't she come with us?" Tessa whispered, glancing back at the woman. "I bet she knows all the good flavors."

"Bye, pretty lady!" Emi yelled.

Twin stabs to his heart, his small beauties. One so careful or in awe of the world that she didn't speak much, and when she did, it was mostly in whispers.

The other was fearless and loud and overflowing with her emotions.

"I bet we can find the good flavors all on our own." *Strawberry, Rocky Road, Butter Pecan.* It might take a list of flavors to get him to chill out. *Keep walking, walk it out.* The fresh air was nice, but damn the heat was relentless today. Sure wasn't a Boston spring, where they'd most likely still be wearing jackets and checking the weather for signs of snow or rain, or both on any given day.

Although, his friend Cruz said it was an odd early heat wave they were having here in Graciella. Either way, today the heat engulfed him...*except it's not the heat, idiot.* Christ, it had been three years. *Why now on some random day?*

"There it is!" Emi ripped her hand from his and took off running.

"Emi wait," he yelled.

She stopped and sighed a sigh bigger than her tiny four-year-old body should be able to produce. "There's no streets. I'm being safe."

"Running away from me isn't being safe."

"I wasn't running *away*, Daddy." She rolled her eyes with the skill of a sixteen-year-old. She pointed. "I'm running *to* that."

Luca caught up to her and opened the door to Unicorn Sweets. It was an ice cream, candy, confectionary explosion of color and smells. Sugar and syrup and more sugar. He was going to be in trouble tonight with twins crashing simultaneously, but taking a huge gulp of cold air, he tossed that thought away to deal with later and gave a tiny sigh of thanks to the inventors of air conditioning and refrigeration. They might have saved him having a full-blown panic attack on Main Street of the town he'd recently moved his daughters to, three thousand odd miles away from their home for a fresh start. On a whim. *Not on a whim – a search for a better life.*

"I want bubblegum. Do they have bubblegum flavor with the real pieces of gum inside? It's two treats for one. That's what I want." Emi stood on her tiptoes and pressed her face into the glass overlooking the flavors.

Tess tugged his hand and he lifted her into his arms. One arm wrapped around his shoulders as far as her little arm could go, and she patted him. He didn't know if it was an instinctive gesture, one he often did to them, or if she was trying to give him comfort, his tiny sage. Or maybe this was her safe place. He liked to believe that.

"No bubblegum, lovelies," a young woman said from behind the counter. "But we do have chocolate with homemade marshmallow sauce. That's my favorite."

Tess hugged him and whispered, "She has pink hair."

Right as Emi demanded, "Daddy, I want pink hair."

The woman behind the counter laughed and said, "Pretty cool, isn't it?" She flipped her hair around and smiled. "Gabby did it. She's the best. I can't wait till she opens her salon."

"Me too." Emi nodded as if she knew who Gabby was.

Luca didn't know whether to be grateful that his daughter was now completely distracted from the no bubble gum ice cream, or afraid of the pink hair chasm he now faced down. His daughters were only four. Didn't he have ten years or so before they demanded pink hair? "Let's start with ice cream," he said.

Emi scowled and he hid the laugh that wanted to bust out of him.

"I'll have the chocolate with marshmallow sauce," Tess whispered to him.

"Me too," Emi said. Luca wasn't certain Emi heard her sister, but it didn't really matter. For as different as they were in many ways, his twins definitely had a strong connection with each other.

"Cones or bowls? I'm Daisy, by the way. Are you visiting or new in town?"

"Bowls," Luca said, as his daughters both chose cones.

"How about if we put it in bowls because then you get more sauce, but I'll top it with a cone, a narwhal horn. That way you get the best of both," Daisy suggested and Luca gave her an invisible high five.

"Yes, please," his girls said. Emi jumped up and down and clapped, Tess hugged him tighter. He led them to a table near the window and returned for their treats.

"Thanks for the cone bowl save," he said and dug out his wallet.

"No problem." Daisy laughed. "I have three younger brothers. I'm also an excellent babysitter if you need one. Here." She handed him his change and a business card with her babysitting info on it. He took the card and stuffed all his change in the tip jar. A babysitter with pink hair who could finagle his daughters into choosing the safer ice cream choice, *and* good business sense? She was a parent's dream sitter.

"Thanks," he said. "We just moved here from Boston. I'm friends with the Brockmans."

"Oh. That's great. My parents grew up with the brothers. Ask any of them about Daisy Gonzales and you should get a great reference for me to babysit."

The bell on the door chimed and she went to help the newcomers.

Luca handed his girls their ice cream. He tossed down his bag that held their sippy cups, a gazillion snacks, minifigures and a change of clothes for each girl. It hadn't taken him long to master the dad diaper bag. *Too bad every parenting decision isn't that easy.* Gulping from his water bottle, he let the cold liquid settle him.

Tess was successfully getting marshmallow sauce all over her fingers, even with the use of the spoon. But her smile was worth it. And Emi was talking a mile a minute while eating. He refrained from saying anything and simply sat with his girls while they ate and giggled, getting messy with their ice cream.

Luca forced himself to take a few deep breaths while the adrenaline ran its course through his blood and the quiet ice cream shop offered him a few moments of peace. Peace, as a single dad of twins, would never last. Peace that just for now he could bask in and ignore visions of dead women lying on the floor.

* * * *

"You're the meanest dad ever," Emi cried as he carried her to bed that night.

"Shh, Emi," Tess said from his other arm. "Don't say bad things."

"It's the truth!"

"Sorry, love. No pink hair for you right now. It's too hard to turn dark hair pink. And you're too young."

"How do you know? I bet Gabby knows. Let's ask her."

We don't even know who Gabby is. He kept that nugget to himself. The meltdown was miserable enough tonight. It was a sign of how tired she was that even in her anger Emi flopped her head on his shoulder. They were both asleep by the time he got them tucked in. Glancing between them in their new twin beds, he hoped like hell he'd made the right decision.

He'd quit everything, his life, his city, his job. *Not everything.* He sighed. Two soft sleeping faces lost in dreamland, *they* were his everything, right here in this room. And he was determined to give them a better life than he *had* been giving them.

Luca tossed the stuffed unicorns and light sabers into the toy bin and made his way to his new back patio with a gorgeous view of the Pacific Ocean. The house needed some work, but he'd loved it immediately, maybe because of the view. The enormous wide-open acres of yard weren't a hardship either. A few fruit trees lined one side, along with an enormous oak that had a perfect branch for a rope swing, maybe even a treehouse.

Lilacs and dogwoods, loads of room for the girls to roam and play, enough scruff and overgrown brambles to give him a good cleanup project and for him to plant whatever he wanted to. Living in Boston and working excruciatingly long hours indoors, he hadn't seen this much grass and this many trees in a long time. His body and his mind had missed it all.

As the sky darkened, the scent of the salty ocean teased some life into him. Exhaustion beat through his muscles, but the night was too perfect not to enjoy. *Not to mention the precious moments of solitude.*

His body might be tired, but his mind opened to what had happened today in town. One minute he and the girls had been peeking through shopfront windows and the next fear had squeezed his heart when he'd seen the woman unconscious on the floor of the empty shop. And what had he done? Jesus, initially he'd frozen, letting his girls get to her first. Then when the blood had rushed back to his head and he realized the woman was simply daydreaming, he'd spit all his old demons onto her, yelled at her then stalked out. *Not your finest moment of being a friendly neighbor. Not by a long shot.*

Three years had passed since that horrible morning when he'd found Noelle's body. And one instant today had dragged him back to that tragedy. Maybe all these drastic changes he'd made in his and his daughters' lives were what had shaken the ghost from its grave. He hoped it wasn't going to be a common occurrence, because, like it or not, big changes were here, and more were about to come. *New beginnings are a good thing.* He believed that with all his heart. He had to.

Plus, Luca could admit to himself under the cover of darkness, while he sat alone, that he was tired of being lonely. He was ready for more.

Chapter Three

"Gabby, I'm so glad you came." Even though she was half a foot shorter than Gabby, Lily's embrace was a monster hug, completely enveloping and wonderful. "You've been home for two months and we still haven't had a good catch-up."

Not for lack of Lily trying. "I know." It was all she could say at the moment, all she was capable of expressing. There was so much silent communication between Lily's words and hers. "I've missed you." *I've missed you so much. You have no idea.* Gabby denied her tears. This was a barbecue, not a cryfest. A perfect crystal-clear day in Graciella with high enough spring temperatures for her best friend, Lily Brockman, to have a pool party. The first one of the season, and the first one Gabby had been to in years.

Lily squeezed her tighter. "Same, Gabs, same. Now tell me what you brought." True to her nature, Lily had moved on from the emotional to the topic of food. Although really the two were closely intertwined for Lily. She stuck her nose in Gabby's bag. "Ahh, I can smell them! Your famous chocolate chip cookies. Oh my gosh, they're still warm. How in the world can something so simple be so damn delicious? One day you'll tell me your secret."

Gabby leaned in and whispered, "Browned butter and way too many chocolate chunks."

Lily's eyes went wide, almost wider than her smile. "You told me."

"I decided those kinds of secrets are more fun to share." It felt good to be here, with her friends and her family. Coming home had been both a balm and difficult. She'd longed for the beauty and comfort of Graciella, but she had so much to mourn as well. And she had friendships to mend, friendships she'd been avoiding.

Lily had done her best to keep in touch when Gabby had been in Los Angeles. And Gabby had reciprocated for a while. But when things had turned sour, betrayal and embarrassment followed by crushing heartbreak, Gabby had pulled inward. She hadn't known how to deal with her life implosion, let alone tell someone else about it. Ironically, it was when she finally sought help from a therapist in L.A. and found a great one that she decided to come home. She was grateful her therapist had agreed to remote sessions for a while.

"You know you can share all your secrets with me." Lily had always been good at reading people's emotions. "Whenever you're ready, honey." Lily squeezed her hand. "We all love you and want to make sure you're okay. We're worried."

"I'm just a little heart hurt, not sick, Lil."

"Some jackass broke your heart. That's still huge, still important."

"I know." *Boy, is Lily right about that.* In the beginning, it had felt like a weird kind of death, one she had to survive every day. She'd been hurt, but mostly what she had to deal with was shame of ever having been fooled by Johnny in the first place, for giving even a tiny bit of herself. She didn't deserve sympathy for that. Gabby squeezed back. "But I'm fine." She wasn't, but she was determined to get there.

"Hmm." Lily narrowed her focus. She might have believed Gabby. More likely she'd wait to ambush later when Gabby least expected it. Gabby gave a tiny sigh of relief it wasn't now. "If you say so. I'll be out in a few minutes after I mix the pasta salad."

Lily gave Gabby a gentle shove toward the backyard. The sliding doors were open to the shimmering, beautiful pool. *Ahh.* Lily's yard alone could be considered therapy.

She waved to her cousin Roxanna and her husband, Miguel, with their big brood of kids, most of whom were in the pool. Lily's husband, Turner Brockman, tossed food on the grill beside Cruz Brockman, who was holding Cruz and Miranda's two-year-old son. He and Miranda had a new baby as well, she'd heard.

Gabby almost hadn't come today. She'd known about all the babies in Graciella — her mom had kept her up to date on all the local gossip. Her heart still hurt, though at the notion of being around couples full of happy-ever-afters and bunches of babies.

"Gabby, come swim with us," her fifteen-year-old cousin, Ana, called to her from the pool.

She didn't see her friends Miranda or Cass yet, so she shed her coverup and dove into the brilliant blue water. It was good. She could splash and play with the kids. So much easier than conversing with adults sometimes, especially in her weird, fragile new state.

Here we go. The last weekend before total chaos began. *Who am I kidding? I have twins and it never gets easier.* The last Saturday in March and it was eighty degrees already. Emi clung to Luca's back, and he held Tess in one arm, their bag of clothes and stuff in the other, while his mind whirred with all the things he had to accomplish tomorrow before he started his new job. So here they were at a barbecue with friends to enjoy one last lazy Saturday. A barbecue, with a pool. The girls clamored down as soon as he made it outside, Emi taking Tess's hand.

"It's the prettiest thing I've ever seen." Emi swooned.

His girl had good taste. Lily Brockman's backyard was stunning. Pink terra cotta walls, with bougainvillea and jasmine vines climbing them, surrounded an oasis. Enormous urns overflowed with plants. A large grassy area surrounded a cement deck and nestled in the middle was a large pool with deep blue Moroccan tiles. An outdoor kitchen sat at one end of the patio off the house. Pool loungers and a long rectangle dining table and chairs were artfully placed. Lights hung everywhere and Luca imagined it would be gorgeous at night too, a fantasyland secluded pool with a Mediterranean vibe.

But Emi was wrong. The pool wasn't the prettiest thing ever. The mermaid with the golden-brown skin playing with the kids in the pool had his heart stirring. A large floral tattoo snaked over one shoulder and down her arm, blues and greens twining together.

"It's the pretty lady from the floor," Tess whispered.

Something tightened in his chest again, but this time it wasn't from fear. The woman wore a simple one-piece brown suit, the simplicity of which only added to her beauty. Water sluiced over her skin as she surfaced, and her smile was unguarded and sparkling under the sunlight.

"She's doing somersaults underwater!" Emi was in awe.

So was Luca. How had he not noticed the woman's smile and the softness of her full lips yesterday? Or her husky laugh as the kids in the pool teased her? Well, mistaking her for dead, then chewing her out, coupled with a panic attack might have slightly gotten in the way of this vision yesterday. He certainly hadn't made her laugh.

"Hi, Luca." Miranda, Cruz's wife, took his bag and set it on one of the chairs. "You made it! Emilia and Tessa—I'm so excited. There are lots of kids here. Even a few around your age. I bet you'll be in the same preschool class."

"Can we swim?" Tess asked Miranda, hardly a whisper at all.

Luca studied his normally quiet daughter, the watchful one. The wistful tone in her voice made that ache squeeze his chest. The one that hit home every time he worried whether he was doing this whole parenting thing right or not, screwing them up one decision at a time. He'd known there was a pool. But he'd somehow hoped it might be raining or lighting or *anything* to keep his girls from wanting to dive in. It had been easy to keep them away from the water in Boston. They were either at daycare or with him and he never deliberately took them anywhere near the shore.

"Of course you can. If it's okay with your dad."

"We don't have swimsuits." *Oh shit.* Emi was on the brink of tears.

Miranda laughed. "Honey, that's okay. All our little ones sometimes swim in their T-shirts and underwear. I also know for a fact Lily keeps extra suits around."

Luca was both horrified and grateful.

"Maybe we can swim with the pretty lady."

"The pretty lady?" Miranda asked and Emi and Tess both pointed. "You mean Gabby?"

"That's Gabby!" Emi squealed. She grabbed Luca's hand and dragged him to the pool edge. She had her sandals kicked off and dress halfway over her head before Luca could stop her. "Gabby!" Emi yelled.

She hovered by him, but he could feel her vibrating to run free right into the water.

"Are you Gabby?" The mermaid and a teenage girl with long black hair and a green and white polka dot swimsuit turned toward them. "Can you make my hair pink like Daisy's?"

"Emi," he said, grabbing Emi's hand, lest she dive right in with her joy. He glanced at Gabby. Her smile was gone, but at least she wasn't looking at him like he was crazy or only had one eye. He raised his hand. "I think we...uh, met yesterday."

"Hmm." She tightened her lips and stood up in the water, coming closer to them, her hands on her hips. Water lapped against those hands and surrounded her waist. "I don't think we actually did. Meet, that is."

"No." He shook his head. His brain was foggy, or his bones. It wasn't panic attack weird. It was something else altogether. Sunlight flickered off the sparks of gold in her brown eyes. "You...I, um, thought you were..." *Dead. Nope.* He cleared his throat. *Can't say that.* "I owe you an apology. I think I was pretty rude."

"You think?" She raised her eyebrow.

Damn. How did women do that, give an entire lecture or reprimand with one sharp eyebrow? Emi was a pro at it too and she was only four.

"I was rude." He managed to squeeze the words through his tightened throat. "And I apologize. No excuse. I'm Luca." See, he could do this, speak actual words to a mermaid. *Woman, she's a woman.*

"Wow, are you twins?" the teenager asked, swimming up beside them.

Emi and Tess turned their attention to her and nodded.

"I'm a twin too. Except my twin is a boy. Are you coming swimming?"

Gabby had never seen a man look more uncomfortable in his life. Yesterday she'd been so shocked by the zap of electricity between them and the pull of his eyes to really be that bothered by his rudeness. He'd whisked himself and his daughters away so fast that she'd questioned whether the whole incident had actually happened.

But here he was, hulking in front of her, blocking her sunshine again and casting that intense cobalt gaze her way. Yesterday he'd spoken and acted angry, but his face had betrayed him. He'd been…afraid. It was shock or fear she'd glanced in his expression before he'd quickly escaped with his daughters.

It wasn't fear now, and it certainly didn't seem like anger. No, he just looked completely out of his element.

"Our daddy's afraid of the water," one of the tiny girls said.

"Emi," he admonished. "I am not."

"How come you never taught us to swim, then?"

"It's because someone drownded a long time ago, Emi." The other twin spoke softly. She also, like her sister, took off her sundress and her sandals. Then she sat at the edge of the pool and dangled her feet in the cool water. "Sit by me." She patted the cement and Emi sat right next to her. "How come your twin is a boy?"

The soft whisper of her tiny voice made Gabby smile and sigh and ache all at the same time.

"Some twins are both girls," Ana said. "And some are both boys, and some are a boy and a girl. Amazing, huh?"

"Yeah, amazing," both little girls said and nodded. They'd twined their hands together, linked themselves as though they were one unit.

"I like your suit," the one he'd called Emi said. She kicked at the water and splashed. Her giggle followed. Leaning her head back, she begged, "Daddy we really, really, really want to swim."

"They can swim with me," Gabby offered. She didn't know why she'd said it. It had sputtered out of her.

"Gabby's great. She taught us all to swim. She was even on a swim team for like forever," Ana said. "I can help too. I'm a lifeguard at the city pool."

Both little girls gazed at Luca with their enormous chocolate brown eyes and Gabby swallowed her laugh. She was absolutely certain he wasn't going to be able to resist their pleas, and she didn't even know him.

"Are you sure?" he asked. *Poor man.* His worry was real, bleeding out of him.

"Honestly." She smiled. "It's no trouble, and it'll be fun. It is awful hot out."

He held her gaze and she felt it again, the link fluttering between them. So much of her wanted to dart away. It was so intense, so serious but she didn't want him to think her a flake, not when it concerned his daughters.

"Okay," he finally said. "One at a time, maybe."

The girls squealed and clapped, and Ana did a backflip to celebrate with them. "Tessa can go first," Emi said, which Gabby found curious. Already she'd pegged Emi as the fearless leader forging into battle, while Tessa seemed calm and content, the observer, maybe.

Tessa patted her dad's leg and whispered, "Thank you." Then she held out her arms to Gabby, her smile a thousand bright stars.

"Ready?" Gabby asked. She wasn't completely certain if she was asking Tess or herself. But there was no time to contemplate as the little girl flung herself into Gabby's outstretched arms...and stabbed at the layers of sadness around her battered heart.

"Hi," Tessa whispered, her eyes meeting Gabby's.

"Hi," Gabby said. "I've got you." Tess patted Gabby on the back, and her heart melted a little more. *Holy crap. Deep breath, Gabby.* "Want to spin?"

Tess gave her a lopsided smile and nodded her head.

"I can help Emi," Ana said. "We'll be careful."

There was a pause and Gabby stole a glance at Luca, who was looking directly at her. "All right," he said, infusing those two words with all the trust in the world.

Before he had the words out, Emi catapulted herself into Ana's arms, splashing up a storm. "I'm gonna love the hell out of swimming," she yelled. There was one second of quiet before everyone around them burst out laughing.

"Emilia Grace," Luca reprimanded.

"Hell is just a word, Daddy, for an imaginary place. Beeeesides, you say hell." She had her arms around Ana's neck and was kicking out uncoordinated splashes with her tiny feet.

"What did I tell you about swear words?"

"They're only for grownups to say."

"And are you a grownup?"

"Maybe."

Gabby couldn't help but laugh at the girl's moxie. She caught Luca's raised eyebrows and a quirk in his lips. Hmm, very full, lush lips that she absolutely hadn't noticed yesterday. *Super sexy when he's trying not to laugh. Nope, not going there. Sexy men – correction, all men – are off limits.* Gabby wondered if he would jump in after his girls. He certainly appeared to be holding himself in check by a very thin thread.

"Come on, take advantage of the break," Miranda said to Luca. "The girls will be fine." Surprisingly he did. And Gabby only stole one glance of him walking away before she turned into the sparkles of swimming with a couple of bright little girls.

Chapter Four

"You're doing pretty well, pal," Cruz said, and lightly smacked Luca on the arm. They sat next to each other in the shade by the pool, Cruz's newborn, Nora, asleep in his lap.

"I am?" Luca asked. He lifted his hat and ran his fingers through his hair. If he had his swimsuit, he'd be in the water right now.

"Well, you haven't leapt in to rescue anyone yet."

"Is it that easy to tell?" Luca tried to relax.

Cruz laughed. "Probably only because I'm a dad with two tiny souls to care for now too. And..." He paused, his voice quieter. "I remember Dominic."

Luca breathed through the emotions welling inside him. Not many people in his life now knew his brother. Cruz had been there that dreadful summer. Luca might not have gotten through that horrible time if it weren't for Cruz, Turner and their friend Jake. "It never goes away," he said softly. "The pain. Missing him."

"I'm sorry, Luca. That summer affected all of us, but none more than you. I can't imagine what it's like to lose a brother, to be here now in life without Turner or Adam." Cruz let the words hang between them for a moment. "Your girls are safe here, and they're having a blast."

"Yeah." Luca sighed. Ana and Gabby both held one of his daughters. They were teaching them how to kick. A skill Luca should have already taught them. Hell, they'd lived on one coast and now another. Their new backyard practically butted up against the ocean. Why in the world had he not taught them how to swim already? Even his mom had encouraged him to. He'd ignored her. His trauma had made him stupid. He'd not only denied them the pleasure, but he'd also been absent in teaching them an important life skill. Dominic's death was a freak accident.

And yet, when they'd first gotten in the water, he'd wanted to pull them back and run. Luckily his irrational behavior hadn't gotten the best of him. His friends had lured him away from the edge of the pool, assuring him that Gabby and Ana wouldn't let anything bad happen. He'd enjoyed adult conversation and a beer without a little person needing him. *Mostly enjoyed.* His fear of them near the water had lessened a bit. His heart, on the other hand, felt like it had had an injection of caffeine. It was the thumping of his heart at seeing Gabby with his girls, which he didn't know how to explain.

Interest in relationships hadn't been on his radar in years. Life as a single parent had been too fucking busy. *Maybe you're afraid to risk love again.* Losing his brother, then losing Noelle... He worked the thought through his mind. He had been afraid. The question ran through his mind, *am I still?*

"Gabby's great with the kids."

"Mm," Luca said. He wanted to ask more about her. Who was she? Where had she come from? Was she dating anyone? And what had she been daydreaming about yesterday on the floor of that building?

"Seriously, Luca, we're all here to help you. I know moving across the country and leaving everything behind is stressful, but you're in a good place. Family, friends, lots of kids for the girls."

"We didn't leave much behind." It was the truth. And that was a relief. He was thrilled to be here. *Should have made the change a long time ago.* Good things were on the horizon.

"Yeah," Cruz said. "I know how that goes."

"I may look crazy when it comes to my daughters in the water, but I'm excited about the move. I appreciate everything you all have done for me, for us."

"Ready for this week?"

"Absolutely. Never been more excited to go to work."

"Nervous?"

"Nope," Luca said confidently. He couldn't wait to get started landscaping again. Christ, not having to work in an office excited the hell out of him. Here he was refreshed and ready to go. "As long as I can get Emi out of the door to preschool without wanting to switch outfits seven million times, things should be fine."

Cruz laughed and stood as his baby started fussing. "Gotta find a bottle. This one's hungry. Glad you're here. We all are." He glanced between Luca and the pool, and a grin broke out on his face. "Oh, an FYI, Rossi, it seems people move here and often find love. Something in the water. No pun intended."

Luca smirked at Cruz and shook his head before the man left in search of a baby bottle. Content to sit alone and watch his girls, he focused on their smiles and laughter, the way Tess sputtered and scrunched up her face when she was splashed, and the absolute delight spread out on Emi's face. *This, this is what I want them to have in life – pure delight, new adventures and connection.*

He could sense Emi getting fatigued when she clung to Gabby and put her head on Gabby's shoulder. That spasm clawed at his heart. It definitely wasn't a sensation he could easily tamp down. He wasn't sure what it was trying to tell him, or what to do with it. He'd upended their lives to give them exactly all this they were surrounded by. Had he ever really intended to find these things for himself too? He'd be a fool to think no, and yet, joy and connection in his past had come with painful tragedy.

Luca was ready with towels when the girls got out. He wrapped Emi in one and sat her in the chair he'd been using, her little teeth chattering. Holding hands, Gabby and Tess walked his way.

"I think they had a blast," Gabby said.

"Yeah, thanks." Luca tried to ignore the way her voice felt swishing against his body, soft and deep. He tried to concentrate on warming his kids and not on how pretty Gabby's wet skin looked in the fading sunlight. And he absolutely avoided staring at the gold loops holding her swimsuit together in the middle of her chest, how sexy her tattoo was, how rosy her cheeks were, how desperately he wanted to run his thumb across those cheeks before he kissed her. It took every single ounce of control he had not to ogle her and drool while doing it.

Shit, his mind was an out-of-control tumbleweed blowing across the desert. What the hell was wrong with him? He scooped up his two burrito-wrapped girls. "Let's get you changed. Then you can sit in the sun and eat a hot dog."

"Need any help?" Gabby asked.

"I've got it."

"Right." She took a step away. Smile gone, a screen slammed shut across her face and she nodded. Then she grabbed her own towel and wrapped it around her body like a cape hiding herself from him.

Quit snarling at the woman.

She turned and started to walk away.

"Thank you," he called. "I..." *I...what?* Where the hell were his words? "Thank you for swimming with them."

She studied him, her face a stoic mask, not one ounce of emotion. "You're welcome. They're lovely."

"Bye, Gabby," both girls said in unison.

"Bye, girls." Her expression softened toward them. "Thank you for swimming with me. It was wonderful."

"Daddy, I'm freezing," Emi said and shivered in his arms.

"Yep, let's go." Watching Gabby walk away, Luca didn't know whether to be glad or regretful. Wasn't a woman the last thing he should be worrying about right now, even one as alluring as her? That thought wormed through his mind as he got the girls dressed. Maybe he could simply try talking to her, have an actual conversation, one where he wasn't being short and rude and biting her head off. But as soon as he came back out with his girls dressed in dry clothes, Gabby was gone.

Chapter Five

Not even a little rain could dampen Gabby's mood this morning as she approached her salon. In fact, she'd missed the rain when she was in Los Angeles. She'd missed all the seasons. Today, she'd donned her denim overalls, held her curls away from her face in short braids and was ready to wield the paint brushes and rollers. Gabby wanted to put her stamp on her salon, feel as though she'd helped it transform, not sat idly by and let other people do it.

She was *sooo* done with letting other people make decisions for her. Ignorance was never bliss as people often said. Ignorance was stupidity and shame and heartbreak.

The door to her salon was propped open and Lily stood on a drop cloth mixing paint.

"What are you doing here? Don't you have five million job sites to manage?"

"Please don't put me in an early grave," Lily said. "It's more like five at the moment. Plus, I have a new general contractor to help manage projects, an absolute perfection in a husband and an amazing crew ready to work. Which means I, the owner, get to help you paint your very own salon today."

"I could swear I told you I was going to do the painting."

"Duh, I know that. But did you really think I was going to let you do it by yourself?"

"Ahh, you're sneakier than I remember," Gabby said.

She set her coffee thermos down and gave Lily a side hug. Lily might have succeeded in ambushing her into long hours of painting, in which Gabby would most likely be forced to talk, but deep in the recesses of her heart, she was grateful. She'd had a hard time making good friends in Los Angeles, people she could really trust. Lily had been her best friend for so long. She was one of the few people Gabby could count on one hundred percent.

"Painting is boring as hell, girl. Perfect for good conversation. Plus, you've been avoiding me. If I didn't ambush you, you might never spill your guts. And you, my love, have so much weighing on you."

Gabby closed her eyes. "It's so hard to know where to begin." She sighed. "Actually, that's not true. It's that I don't want to begin."

"I know, but maybe it will feel good to talk about things. I missed the hell out of you. You disappeared in California. I'm so happy you're home, but...I...I still miss you."

Gabby bit back the tears. She was home, but she'd been hiding.

"Start with Jackass Johnny. I never liked him."

"You never met him."

"I know," Lily said, exasperated. "That's part of the problem. I never met the piece of scum who broke your heart!"

Lily didn't mean it as a slam, but it hurt. Gabby deserved it. "I'm sorry, Lily. I'm so sorry. I got swept up in things when I moved there to finish my training. The pressure was so intense. I was all by myself and way out of my league, neither of which I anticipated or really knew how to deal with it turns out. And he was brash and bold and strong, everything I wanted to be."

"You mean everything you *are*," Lily said.

Not anymore. "I'm not sure about that."

"What?" Lily spun on her. "What are you talking about? You're this rainbow explosion of colorful bravery with all the shimmery gold at the end. Which reminds me, why are we painting everything white again?" Lily studied the walls.

Gabby grabbed a roller and furiously attacked the drywall with the bright paint as if that action alone could wipe out her failed relationship. It sucked, remembering the thrill of what she'd thought was love. How she'd ignored or just flat-out hadn't seen so many signs that said she should slow the hell down and pay attention.

"He was wonderful in the beginning, or he seemed that way. Kind of like fake bling you know, without much substance beneath. Or all the wrong substance, I started to discover." White stripes of paint covered the drywall as Gabby moved the roller.

"Did he hurt you?" Lily's voice was a whisper.

Gabby stopped painting. She stared at the wall and felt the pain pulsing from her friend. *No more than any of the other guys who dumped me,* she lied to herself.

"No, honey. I'm sorry if I ever let you think that." She'd made so many mistakes, but ignoring her friendship with Lily had been one of the biggest. Pausing, she faced her. "Not how you mean. I think he wanted me to be different. He'd frame his gifts as things that were better than what I already had. He'd make suggestions about what I should wear, what food I should eat. All cased in having my best interests at heart. I don't know why I couldn't see it in the beginning. I was so overwhelmed and..." *Lonely, Starved for attention.* "A tiny part of me thought maybe if I did change, he, *any guy* would stick around.

"He wanted me to be someone else, someone less than him, as it turned out. Oh, and of course I wasn't the only woman in his life." There she'd said it. It was out there in the space between them. The shame slicked against her skin, how it always did when she remembered.

"What the fuck?" Lily truly could go from heartbroken and worried for her to an inferno of rage in seconds. "I don't know which is worse, trying to change you, or... He cheated? On *you?*" Lily painted her fury out on the wall. One big huffy tornado. "It's a damn good thing I never met the slimy ball of flesh, because I would chew him up and spit him out, then light him on fire and watch him burn, slowly, in agony. No fucking mercy at all."

Gabby was laughing by the time Lily finished her rant, and it eased the pain around her heart a bit. "That is some very specific rage."

Lily pinned Gabby with her serious gaze. "He doesn't deserve to breathe the same air. He *did* hurt you. Maybe not physically. But he broke your heart and made you doubt yourself." Lily flung down her paint roller and used a clean paint rag to wipe her tears.

"Come here." Gabby wrapped her arms around Lily.

But Lily struggled and wrapped her arms around Gabby. "No, I'm not the one who needs a hug, you are. Do you hear me?" A few minutes later they were tickling and laughing through their tears.

Gabby was grateful for the morning. Lily was right, it did feel good to talk to her best friend. Some of her weight had been lifted. She hadn't told her the most difficult thing, but it could wait. *Maybe for forever.*

* * * *

Her shoulders and wrist ached already. Apparently, it didn't matter how much yoga one did — painting was its own form of torture. But Lily was right about it being a good environment for talking. Painting had also been great for getting some stress out. Lily left to get them some late lunch and Gabby was determined to finish the one wall she'd been working on. She cranked up her music, hoping it would drown out the dreadful construction noise from outside. Eventually, she couldn't take it any longer. The pounding overwhelmed the beat of her music.

Luca Rossi wielded a jackhammer and was currently destroying a part of her wide sidewalk. For a few seconds on Saturday, she'd almost thought him sexy and cute, but his short, clipped demeanor toward her had quickly obliterated that.

Her side of the street was blocked off and orange spray paint rectangles were sprayed along the sidewalk. Piles of rubble existed where he'd already been. Two men cleared the rubble farther down the block. She waved to get his attention. "What are you doing?" she yelled.

He still had his headphones on, and his eyes were covered in safety goggles. Not one inch of his face cracked into a smile. Was the jerk even capable of one? But all his focus was directed at her. Definitely something in the air—a thick humid cloud surrounded her.

He paused like he'd done at the BBQ on Saturday, eyes never leaving hers. Well, at least that was a change. Most men needed help lifting their eyes off her chest. Slowly, he pulled the headphones off. "Pardon?"

"What are you doing to my sidewalk?"

"*Your* sidewalk?"

Ooo, this idiot could ruffle her feathers with fewer words than a mime. And look sexy doing it. *No, no, no, he's not sexy.* There was nothing sexy about rudeness, and there was absolutely no sexy in her life right now anyway. "Yes." One hand on her hip she pointed down with the other, trying very hard not to stab it at him. "This sidewalk in front of my salon."

Luca studied her with such heat that she felt it lick along her bones, weave its way into her thoughts, her emotions. *Old hat on backward, dark stubble along his stoic jaw, T-shirt plastered to his skin from rain or sweat.* Who knew? She'd only seen him in shorts before, but today he was in long worn blue jeans. Mm, if only she could see what they did to his butt. Large arm muscles wielding the enormous jackhammer. How did one hold that thing anyway? *With those gorgeous arm muscles, and those strong, sexy hands. That's how. Lord.* She took a deep breath. He was like an annoying gnat, and she stood here objectifying him and his hotness.

"Could swear it belongs to Graciella."

Huh, there was his smile, barely. One side of his lips tipped up. He raised his eyebrows slightly above the safety glasses as if he was... *Is he making fun of me?* Gabby rubbed the headache worming its way through her temples. *Why, why me?*

Luca wasn't sure what it said about him that he enjoyed sparring with this woman. Working the jackhammer was his least favorite part of the job, but they needed to dig up sections of cement before the new planters could be set in place. He had a very small crew to begin with and he'd need to hire more people, but for now, getting Main Street beautified for the Blossom Festival next month was his main priority.

Focus when using the jackhammer was key, but she'd stepped into his line of sight and distracted him with her inquisition voice and her cute overalls. Paint streaked across her rosy cheek. He had to admit, he didn't mind the distraction at all. But as cute as she was, behind the paint, frustration lined her face.

"Don't worry. I'm only destroying small sections to install new planters. The city is my first client with my new business, Rossi Landscape Design. I promise it won't be a disaster for long."

Her face softened the tiniest bit at his words, and he noted that for later. *Definitely not in the mood for teasing right now. Got it. You haven't really been that nice to her at all, during any of your interactions.* That dug under his nail like a splinter. He'd been raised better. Being respectful and kind were two things his mom had drilled into him and his brother.

Luca set the machine aside and removed his work gloves. "Seems we haven't really had a friendly official meeting. All my fault. I apologize again. Maybe we could start over." He held out his hand. "Luca Rossi."

She hesitated and he wondered if she'd simply turn and walk away.

"Gabby Flores." She put her hand in his and the heat of it melted right through his tough skin and catapulted him into space. He had to physically restrain his arm so it wouldn't tug her right into his body.

Where she belongs. Whoa, buddy. Slow down.

"You…uh… live here in Graciella?" she asked, staring at their hands.

"Yes. My girls and I moved here about a month ago. I've known Cruz and Turner for years. We…ah worked summers together during college." Damn, he hadn't babbled to a woman in a long, long time. Had he ever really? Confidence wasn't something he normally lacked.

"Oh." She didn't say much, even less with her expressions. He liked it better when her temper was up because he was destroying her sidewalk. But he sure enjoyed holding her hand.

"It was really nice of you to swim with Tess and Emi. I didn't thank you properly. They haven't quit gushing about it."

"Gabby, Luca! Two of my favorite people." His good friend Jake Cooper walked up to them, dressed for work in a million-dollar suit, his old worn leather shoulder bag he'd had way back when they were in college slung across his chest.

"Jake. Hey, man…" Luca's words fizzled out as Gabby whisked her hand out of his and was wrapped in an enormous hug from Jake. An unkind feeling tugged in his gut seeing his best friend holding Gabby. The expression on her face was one of joy and delight.

He wanted that look for himself. *Hold on, idiot, you just met her and you've mostly been an ass.*

"You made it to Graciella," Jake said to him, slinging his arm over Gabby's shoulder. "I was just going to call you this afternoon. I'd hug you but you look like you're wearing cement dust. And you're finally back, Gabby. Now *I* just need to find a house here."

"You're looking here?" Gabby squealed. "To buy, like for good?"

"Yep. I have my eye on one of the old Sears Roebuck houses on Emerson Street."

"Awesome. Only now we'll have to figure out how to deal with the hordes of women following you," Gabby teased and poked Jake in the side.

"Hey." He pivoted out of her reach. "I have one girlfriend, singular."

"Mm, hmm. Is this a new one, or the same one you had when I left for California?"

"Uh…new…I think. Whatever." He smirked, a huge grin on his face. "Luca, I have presents for the girls — can I stop by one night this week?"

"Absolutely." Good, he sounded normal through the idiotic snake of jealousy lodged in his throat. "I'll text you our new address as soon as I'm done here."

"Hi, Jake." Lily walked toward them.

"Hey, gorgeous." Jake leaned in and kissed her cheek. "Gotta get to work."

"Sure, sure, you big flirt. Try not to flirt with your clients," she yelled after him as he disappeared around the corner. "I hear that's bad for business. Luca! Yay first day. How's it going?"

"Great," he said. "Assuring Gabby I won't leave her sidewalk in a pile of rubble." He had been calmly doing that before his insides decided to melt down and act like a five-year-old. Now he didn't quite have a grasp on what the hell he was doing.

"Luca's my new partner, Gabby. Isn't it so exciting? I've been dreaming of a landscape design partner for years. The city hired us to put in gorgeous planters all along the street and hanging baskets from the antique lanterns. Right in time for the Blossom Festival to be rejuvenated. Can you believe it's been twenty years since we had a festival? And you're on the festival committee. I'm so excited. Oh, I love new beginnings!"

"Me too," Gabby and Luca said in unison. Luca laughed. Gabby frowned and took a step back.

"Well, I'd better get back to work," he said. "Ladies." Jesus, what did it say about him that he thought her frown was as cute as her smile?

Lily wrapped her arm around Gabby's waist. They walked away and Luca hoped maybe Gabby might glance at him one last time. But she didn't. She disappeared into her shop and shut the door behind them. He'd only wondered a thousand times since Saturday if he had time for a relationship. Right now, his emotions were flipping over in interest for her. And maybe he wasn't disappointed at all. Maybe time had absolutely nothing to do with it. Maybe time could fly right out of the window.

Chapter Six

"Mind if I sit here?"

Gabby shut her sketchbook and looked up. She blinked at the man standing over her. Luca Rossi, *again*. *Seriously?* Only this time *not* wearing a baseball hat or sunglasses. Unruly lush black hair that he'd tried to comb back framed his face. Then there were those deep blue eyes she could swear were trying to unlock all her secrets. A touch of vulnerability streaked through his expression. She caught her breath. *He is so gorgeous. Mm, and he smells good.* Soap and something else she couldn't place...fresh dirt? *No. How can dirt smell good on a man?*

"Let's get started, people," Nina, their city planner, called to the group.

"Uh, no...sure," Gabby stuttered. Luca pulled the chair out and sat right next to her.

"You're an artist?" he asked.

"Huh?" Gabby glanced around the room. What was happening? She was at the meeting for those on the festival committee. He tapped on her book. Gabby tugged it closer to her. "What are you doing here?"

When he smiled, she wasn't ready for it. How it softened the planes of his face, created laugh lines around his mouth, and how even his eyes swirled with some lovely emotion. Those blue depths were trying to lure her in. "Nina thought it would be a good idea if I was here since a large part of the preparation for the festival falls in my hands."

"Uh-huh." She nodded, resting her chin on her hand and watching the words come out of his mouth. Until he quirked those lips of his in that barely there crooked grin, with his eyebrow tipped up again, and this time she knew that grin meant he was mocking her.

Embarrassment flooded her cheeks. She hated that feeling. Nerves turned to sludge in her belly. She shrugged herself out of her Luca Rossi haze, scooted her chair in and sat up straight. Damn, for someone determined to avoid men for a while, she was failing miserably.

"Gabby? Did I say—"

"The meeting's starting," she said.

"Thank you all for coming," Nina began. "I'm so excited for the festival. Many of you have lived here long enough to remember when Graciella had the festivals. As I only moved here last year, I'm excited to be a part of this town's rejuvenation with spring and new beginnings. I invited Luca Rossi tonight as well. He's new in town and his company will be working with Dragonfly Construction and Design to help get our streets and sidewalks beautified for the festival. Gabby, since you're in charge of this year's overall theme, you'll be working with Luca on this. He'll also be in charge of acquiring most of the flowers we'll use for the festival."

You have got to be kidding me. Isn't it bad enough I have to see him flexing outside my salon for the foreseeable future? Now I have to work with the man? Gabby wanted to bang her head on the table, but she was trying to maintain her professionalism.

"Can I ask what the theme is for the festival? It'll help me organize what to include in some of the plantings." He had a nice voice. She'd give him that. When he wasn't being a jerk. He rested his arm on the table, slightly brushing against hers.

"Gabby?" Nina asked.

"It's...I...I thought we'd go with a Pretty in Pink theme as I really want to highlight the whites and pinks of the apple blossoms, all the pink hues of peonies and everything else that will be in bloom then."

Luca let out a deep, sexy chuckle. She closed her eyes. Her cheeks heated with red. *How dare he?* Anger burned inside her along with the shame. *No, no, no,* she reprimanded herself. When was she going to quit doing that, being embarrassed for someone else's shortcomings? When she glared at him, the only part of him left smiling were his eyes. It really was a shame that someone so handsome's best trait was acting like an annoying younger brother pulling her pigtails and pretending it wasn't him.

"I like it," he said. "Great idea. Perfect for this time of year with what will be blooming, as Gabby said. And I can definitely add to her design with the new landscaping along the sidewalks."

Wow. Even more annoying, he could act as if he hadn't just laughed in her face and made fun of her idea.

"Great," Nina said. "Now let's talk timeline for the next few weeks. Then we'll move on to entertainment."

Great, Gabby echoed. *The sooner this meeting finishes, the sooner I can get away from another jackass in my life.*

* * * *

"Gabby, wait." She rolled her eyes and kept walking. She was done waiting for idiotic men who couldn't be respectful. She might be done with men completely. "Gabby, please."

Oh fine. Apparently, she couldn't wish the man away. "Yes." She infused the word with her best haughty tone.

"Something happened in there. I said or did something…I'm not sure what, but…"

She turned away. She wanted to say, *"It was nothing."* It was so much easier. Then she could flee.

"You…I…you sort of shut down on me. Like someone stole the best piece of candy you were saving for last."

But it wasn't *nothing.* It never was. And she'd ignored slights with Johnny the Jackass because she hated confrontation, and because…because she'd been lonely. How pathetic that she'd traded loneliness for emotional manipulation. Those who knew her thought she was bold and brave, but something had happened to her in L.A. She'd been easily intimidated and *so* not brave, especially when out of her element. She'd let someone take advantage of her. But as hard as it was to stand up for herself, she never again wanted to hit the low place she'd found herself in with Johnny.

"You laughed at me." She turned to face him fully, trying to rediscover her bravery, trying to camouflage the shaking in her voice.

"What? No." He shook his head.

"When I announced my theme."

"Oh," he said. Then that devastatingly dangerous full smile took over his face. He slid his hands into the pockets of his shorts and chuckled again. Boy, did she want to wipe that smirk off his face. Or kiss it off. There was a fine line between anger and lust, she found at that moment. But she was done mixing gaslighting and attraction. Gabby shook her head and started toward her car.

Stubborn bastard caught up with her. "I wasn't laughing at you, honestly. I was imagining Emi's squeal of delight when I tell her about the Pretty in Pink theme." He rushed the words out. "She'll think it was named especially for her. Ever since the other day, when we uh…saw you on the floor. We met Daisy, and she told us you did her hair, I've had to talk Emi off the cliff of pink hair."

Oh. One of the ties around Gabby's heart unwound. Her anger slid away. He had so much love in him when he talked about his daughters. She'd never thought of that as an attractive trait.

"It's beyond her favorite color. It's more of an obsession." He took one step closer and as tall as she was, Gabby still had to look up to meet his eyes. "I wasn't laughing at you. Promise."

The seriousness of his expression, the way his eyes got hooded and the lines that wrote their way across his forehead were arguably hotter than his casual smile. Absolutely one hundred percent focused on her. And when he spoke the word promise to her in that sexy soft way he had of apologizing or assuring, she almost melted right there on the pavement.

Gabby took a step back. She put her hand to her cheek, feeling the flush attack her skin as though she'd never been aroused before. *Girl, get it together. Successful, single and fabulous. What part of* single *can't you understand?*

"What's your favorite?" he asked. "Color, that is, not obsession."

Such a simple question, but how close he stood and the way his voice stroked across her skin when he set all his focus on her, it sounded like he'd asked her what color her panties were. It sounded exactly like he wanted to know her obsession.

"Uh, blue?" She swallowed, completely lost in his eyes. "No." She shook her head. "I mean green?"

He tilted his head in confusion. "You sure about that?"

If she hadn't been so focused on his eyes, she might have missed the way he furrowed his brows and studied her. "Yes." She nodded and started to unlock her car. "Green. I'm sure. It's very green. It's been green for a long time."

"Want to get a drink?" he asked.

Gabby rubbed her eyes. She couldn't do this, not now. Not after everything that had happened in California. She was barely standing on her own two feet. The absolute last thing she needed, *wanted* was to get involved with someone. She still had friendships to repair, her own soul to nurture back to health.

"I can't. I don't date." Well, that sounded harsh and also ridiculous. *Who says that? Even if it is the truth.*

"Sorry," he said, stepping away. "I...uh meant so we could talk about your plans and my responsibilities to help...um bring your vision to the festival." He cleared his throat. "There wasn't much time in the meeting, and I thought it would help me to get a better idea of your thoughts."

And I'm the idiot. Even more reason not to get involved right now. She couldn't tell when a man was asking her out or asking about a work function. "Right. I'm sorry. I can't tonight. I have to go." She closed herself in her car and slowly drove away, avoiding all her instincts to look back.

What a mess I still am. I'm running away after all because I'm such a coward.

Even as she drove off and the chances of them getting that drink blew off in a cloud of smoke, Luca backed away as if to put more distance between them, get his head on straight. He *had* meant it exactly the way she'd thought, one person attracted to another, impulsively asking them out. But the look of terror on her face had him changing tactics rapidly. He wasn't sure what he'd been thinking anyway.

That was the problem. He hadn't been thinking or worrying or cataloging all the things he had to get done. He'd simply been enjoying getting lost in her. The light in her eyes she tried to keep hidden, the warm soft brown tones of her skin, and the bright red nail polish she'd painted her fingernails, including something sparkly on her pinkies, a design of some sort. He wanted to know what that design was. He wanted to study the flush that reddened her cheeks when she was upset. *Or maybe attracted.*

Shit. He shook his head. He could tell himself over and over to be cautious about starting a relationship, but it seemed his body had other ideas, commanding control over his brain whenever she was in close proximity to him. Who was he kidding, he'd been thinking about her all week, even when she wasn't standing right in front of him.

Luca still had an hour of babysitting time banked and he was absolutely going to take advantage. Besides, his girls had hardly noticed him leaving once Daisy had arrived with her markers and art kit. He followed the scent of pizza coming from Donny's Pizza Pie. Entering, he was hit with some of the best scents anywhere in the world, a pizza oven, tomato sauce, garlic. *Mm.* He'd have to bring the girls here. They'd love this place, homey, comfortable, full of families, but for tonight he'd find an empty seat at the bar…

"Rossi!" Turner waved him over from one of the booths. "Hey," he said as Luca approached. "I'm waiting for Lily. Want to join us for dinner?"

Luca slid into the booth across from Turner. "No way I'm going to barge in on your date night."

"Have a glass at least. Tell me how your week's been so far." Turner poured him some red wine.

"Fantastic. Busy, but different from the rat race in Boston."

Luca waved a server down and ordered a large pepperoni to go. "The girls love school and Daisy's babysitting tonight. I'm not even sure they cared that I left. Just came from the meeting with the city about the Blossom Festival."

"That's right. Can't believe it's been so long." A grin spread over Turner's face.

"Fond memories?"

"Well, it is a great place to sneak kisses behind all the booths, to romance someone."

Lily swooshed in then and planted a smacking kiss on Turner's lips. "Who are you talking about romancing?" She slid in next to Turner and linked her hand with his on the table.

"You, of course."

Luca couldn't help but be swept up in Lily's smile. She was practically glowing under Turner's gaze.

"Sorry I'm late. New client meeting ran over."

"Did they fall in love with you?"

"Of course they did. You know it. And I love their project. It's the old Fraiser Barn. They want me to turn it into their home. Luca, the landscaping budget for this is huge. Wait until you see it. How was the festival meeting?"

Interesting. "Great," he lied.

Lily's eyes got wide as if her superpower was reading his mind. "You get to work with Gabby, don't you?"

He'd finished his sip of wine, or he might have choked on it. He nodded.

"Oh, goody. I bet her ideas were spectacular. This festival is going to be awesome. This kind of project is right up her alley. Did she show you her drawings for it? I bet her sketchbook is bursting with sparkling ideas.

"She uh, didn't. Nope. The meeting didn't last long, and she had to be somewhere."

"Huh." Lily slumped in the booth. "I was so hoping this festival might kick her out of her funk."

"Lily," Turner said. "She's..." He glanced at Luca.

"I know. She went through a lot. I just want her to be happy." Her voice was hushed as she gazed at Turner.

Luca's pizza arrived then and once again he found himself in the presence of two people who might not notice when he left, so engrossed in each other were they. He couldn't help but smile. His friend Turner had been a broody angst-filled guy in college, and even worse after college when he'd practically disappeared for a decade. It was nice to see him in love and happy with a partner who was perfect for him. He deserved it.

I want that someday.

"Gotta get home to the girls. Thanks for the wine, you two. Have a good night."

Lily tore her attention from Turner and gave him a smile. "Luca, sorry, sometimes my mouth gets ahead of me. Forget I said anything about Gabby. I'll see you tomorrow."

He lifted his chin and grabbed his pizza. On his way home he took a short detour, driving through the city streets to let his mind wander. He wasn't sure he could do what Lily had asked. He now had a few more pieces of Gabby Flores, and he didn't know what that meant or how those tidbits fit the rest of her, but he wanted to know. He wanted to uncover the entire intriguing picture.

That's going to be difficult considering she is one hundred percent not interested.

Chapter Seven

It was amazing what a week could do. Gabby almost twirled around her salon. Painting was finished and the space gleamed white. Stations were in along with the manicure tables. While she waited for the installation of her salon chairs, she finished hanging the curtains she'd bought, white linen as planned. And this afternoon the plumber would be here to install all the sinks. Lily had delivered the large French antique reception desk this week. Gabby found a soft cloth to wipe it down with.

It might have been large and imposing, except that whoever built it had carved in delicate scrollwork across the front and along the sides, giving it an old-world charm. It was made out of pine but had been distressed over the years with an almost silvery white stain. The grain of the wood still shined through, but it had a touch of princess to it.

Gabby paused and studied it. This wasn't in her new plans. Nope, she'd specifically steered clear of dreamy, princessy things. *Maybe I should buy a new modern reception desk, something sleek and unobtrusive that would meld into the décor.* Ugh. She rubbed her chest. That thought didn't sit well with her. She started to shove the uncomfortable feeling away. *Ignoring your instincts is what got you in trouble in California.* The problem was she didn't know what her instincts were telling her right now. She'd lost her way to trusting herself.

"Don't you want to be sophisticated?" Johnny had hinted more than once. According to him, sparkly was nothing but a little girl's dream. *Oh shit, am I designing a salon around what he would think?*

Gabby's butt hit the pretty rattan stool she'd bought for the reception area as that thought knocked the breath out of her. She dragged out her fine black pens and sketchbook. It was one she'd had before she left for California. She'd taken it with her, as she'd always taken her sketchbooks with her in life. But she hadn't drawn in it while she'd been there, not once. When she returned, she'd left several pages blank and started in on her new ideas for her sophisticated salon.

Now she was stuck, hovering between her old dreams and her battered heart.

Ever since she was a little girl, she'd dreamed of having her own salon. She wanted to make people feel as though they were special like they deserved to look spectacular. And she was damn good at it. Correction, she *had* been good at it. Two years of her life down the drain and it felt like eons. And she didn't know how to get that loss back.

"Morning."

Gabby snapped her head up and her book closed at the same time. Then she tried really, really hard not to roll her eyes. "Mr. Rossi," she said as she stood. The man was everywhere.

"Ouch." He winced. "Luca, please. Mr. Rossi was my grandfather, and the only things I remember about him were his temper and his yellowed mustache from too much cigarette smoke."

How was he able to annoy and fluster her in the same space in a matter of seconds? And spark her curiosity? "Just your grandfather?"

"Pardon?" He looked at her in confusion.

"I mean, what about your father? Wasn't he also Mr. Rossi?" She should have reciprocated his good morning and been done with him, shoved him out of the door, returned to her...*to what, my pity party?* But although his interruption may have annoyed her, his voice was a caress, a soft waterwall she wanted to step into, have it wash away all her sins.

Luca's smile dimmed. He always maintained eye contact with her when they spoke. She found it unnerving because it felt like he could see everything inside her, but it also lent him an air of confidence in the sense that he was trustworthy, solid. As if there were no manipulation games going on behind her back. "My father was never in the picture. My mom raised us herself."

"I'm sorry...Luca. That must...it must have been difficult to grow up without a father."

He let out a sigh and leaned his arm on the reception desk, acting completely comfortable and casual, as if they were old friends. "Don't think I minded it as a child. My brother and I were tight and my mom was great. It wasn't until I got older, until...well, when I realized I didn't have much support to lean on when things...were difficult. You know?"

"Mm," she said. "I can appreciate that." *It's one of the biggest reasons I moved home.* What made her want to spill all her deep dark secrets to this stranger? Something held her back. Fear, maybe, or smarts. She'd exposed herself in California and had gotten badly burned for it. She was still licking her wounds.

"Sorry, I didn't mean to get maudlin on you. Your door was open and..."

"No more concrete to destroy?" She certainly didn't want to linger in the sad and heavy, or anything too personal.

"He chuckled. All done. I promise it'll look great when we're finished. In fact, I'm installing the new planters and I had a few minutes. I thought maybe we could talk about the festival or schedule a time. I definitely need your input before I go ahead. You're the expert. I can work around your schedule. Whatever's best for you."

"Oh, right, sure." *Dammit. He's so considerate.* Gabby dug through her bag and pulled out a mostly finished sketch. She'd put her ideas on paper, not in her sketchbook where anyone could filter through the pages and find fault with her. "I drew a little of what I was thinking."

She'd always been better able to show someone her ideas than to tell them. Maybe he could take her drawing and work from there. Maybe they wouldn't have to meet and talk about it. Maybe she wouldn't get lost in the waves of azure in his beautiful eyes.

"Wow." Luca held the paper and took in her designs with his eyes as well as his hands, running his fingertips over it as if were real. "You say a helluva lot with a picture."

He flicked his gaze to hers then back to her drawing. "I love the idea of stringing apple blossoms across the street, interspersed with the small lights in a crisscross pattern. I can attach some tall wooden columns to each of the planters that can be removed after the festival, or become permanent if the city decides they want to keep the lights year-round.

"We could wrap them with blossoms too. Or, if you want, hanging baskets down the sides with different flowers. I can get plenty of peonies, by then, and possibly some leftover tulips. The entrance you've drawn looks amazing as well, with enormous buckets of flowers overflowing. I've got some super pink calla lilies, and of course tons of rhododendron blooms. This is a work of art in itself." He gently tapped her sketch. "You've nailed it. Answered all my questions before I got a chance to ask."

Why did he sound bummed that he hadn't gotten that chance? And why did she suddenly?

"Mind if I keep this?"

"I…" Gabby looked at her drawing in his hands. Suddenly she felt more vulnerable than if he'd seen every page in her book.

"No worries, I'll take a picture with my phone, if that's all right?"

"No, you can take that one. It's fine." She fumbled through her answer.

A few of Lily's employees walked through the door at that moment, saving her. "Hi, Gabby. We're here to get your chairs installed."

"Oh, great. They're in the back. I thought I'd let you all unpack them, so I didn't ruin anything. I'll…uh…" She glanced at Luca.

"Right, I need to get to work too. It's looking good in here, lots of...uh..."

She made the mistake of glancing at him. Intense focus lined his face while he cast his gaze around her salon.

"A lot of white for someone who imagined a Pretty in Pink theme for the city?" His voice was quieter, almost a murmur as if he was talking to himself, his eyebrows furrowed in contemplation.

"It's sleek and clean." Gabby held her sketchbook to her chest. "Exactly the design I'm going for," she said, defense lacing her tone.

"Yes. Right, sorry. I didn't mean any offense." He studied her for a few seconds. Then he gave her a soft smile.

A smile she wanted to tear apart and investigate because she felt as though he were saying something *more* with it, something meaningful and she didn't know what.

"Love this piece, here." He tapped the reception desk. "Great character. Bet it has an amazing history, lots of story behind it, passion and intrigue." He winked at her. "Have a good day, Gabby. I'll get started with your ideas."

Gabby stared at the space he'd been standing in for a long while after he'd left. Her hands shook with nerves, with embarrassment, or something else altogether...an urging? It was harder to understand the difference.

Opening her book, she flipped through the pages. In her old designs, color burst from the pages, orange and purple and yellow flowers lining the edges like gilded frames. She'd drawn loads of people with edgy hairstyles in a rainbow of hues, for men and women, a few children, even her brother Javvie's pink buzz cut when he'd been in high school. Colors and styles that made people happy. More than that, the pages were an explosion of imagination. They were her creations.

The white spaces she'd deliberately left between then and now as if to separate herself completely from the old Gabby or remind herself of how stupid she'd been in California, taunted her. Her new ideas were sterile marks on the page. Today she couldn't find comfort in her new ideas. Something was missing. They were so sparse. *Boring* was the word that whispered through her brain. They were quite a contrast to her earlier designs. One might even call them lifeless, which was much worse than boring. *Hollow.* It was that pain again inside her, that feeling snaking low in her gut. *Hollow.*

"A lot of white for someone who imagined a Pretty in Pink theme for the city?"

Once, long ago, she'd been an absolute artist for hair, wild and bold and overflowing with colorful imaginings. Absolutely sure of herself and unconcerned one iota with what other people thought of her, of her art. She'd lost that part of herself. And she didn't know how to rediscover it. Worse, suddenly it felt like she was the only one holding herself back. The worst betrayal of all.

Chapter Eight

We sure work the hell out of an assembly line. Luca kept the swear word thought to himself but smiled at his little family. Seven a.m. on Saturday morning. The day was going to be another warm one. The scent of dew evaporating off plants and wet dirt infused his senses. Tess and Emi stood in the red wagon to give them a boost. Emi handed Tess the strawberry pots and Tess arranged them on the long wooden table. All this after Luca priced each pot.

"They're so pretty. I love strawberry plants." Emi sighed and caressed the leaves of a Hood strawberry. His favorite by far, smaller berries and super sweet, like candy. He suspected it would be Emi's favorite too.

The nursery he now owned had gotten a huge shipment of new plants early this morning and it was all hands on deck to get things priced and set out for the customers. Having to be here at the crack of dawn was no problem with two little girls who deemed it their duty to never *ever* sleep in on the weekends. The girls had been going strong for half an hour, each one super concentrating on their task. He was lucky that they loved helping him when it came to gardening and plants. Most likely he had about ten minutes of their time left before they were distracted or tired or hungry or wanted to go play on the little playground around back.

Buying the nursery right before he'd gotten out here had also been a last-minute decision, but he couldn't say a bad one. In fact, discovering that it was for sale exactly when he'd decided to move here and start his own landscape business seemed downright fortuitous. An asset he absolutely couldn't turn down, for his business for sure, but also for time to spend with his girls doing something they all loved.

The fact that he'd piled onto his responsibility didn't bother him if this was what he got in exchange. Most likely the girls' serenity wouldn't last, but any chance he got to be outside with them, talking and learning about plants, he considered a win-win. He'd bribed them with a visit to their new favorite ice cream shop later and he couldn't tell if they were more excited for the sweet treat or to see their new pink-haired babysitter, Daisy.

Emi and Tess were dressed in their matching purple T-shirts with an enormous pink daisy on the front, pink shorts and pink canvas tennis shoes. Tess preferred all shades of blue, but once in a while, she let Emi dictate what they'd wear. Although more subtle in her attempts, Tess also wanted to impress Daisy in her own quiet way. They both sported baseball hats, his decision, to guard against the sun.

Early customers meandered around the outdoor area where veggie starts and tons of perennials and annuals sat ready and waiting for a new home. He took a moment to observe and was grateful a joyful staff from the previous owners had wanted to keep their jobs. Hiring for his landscape business *and* staff for the nursery could have provided an enormous obstacle, but the nursery was humming along seamlessly. He was the one getting an education, getting trained.

He spotted young José and Ana, Roxanna and Miguel's twins. For now, they only worked a few hours, but their knowledge of trees and native plants that thrived in this area surpassed Luca's. He needed to talk to them about joining his landscape business as soon as they turned sixteen, which from what he'd heard was next month. Both of them would be huge assets this summer once school was out, if they were interested.

"My goodness, the peonies."

"Mami, you don't need any more peonies."

Luca's gaze traveled over his daughters' heads to see Gabby pushing one of the big carts. It was half full already with a few vegetables and some soil amendments.

"Ha, a lady can never have too many peonies."

"Yes, but you also need a place to put them. And you have zero garden left." Gabby fingered the lime green hellebore, flitted her pretty painted nails over the jagged-edged petals of some near black tulips and leaned in to smell purple hyacinth.

And yet her salon is colorless?

"Ladies," Luca said as they turned down the strawberry aisle.

Gabby glanced up from under her broad sunhat. Confusion, nope, *annoyance* washed over her face before she shuttered everything away again. "Are you following me?" she asked, then pursed her lips as if she hadn't meant to blurt that out.

Hmm, maybe she hadn't shuttered everything. There was some emotion there, banked though it was. He could sense it simmering under the surface. *I wonder why she wants to hide it all.* He sure was wondering a hell of a lot about Ms. Flores lately.

It had only been two days since he'd spoken with her in her shop. He'd intended to get more clarification for the festival. Secretly, he'd wanted to see her. In the end, he'd insulted her. Still hadn't figured out how, though. He was definitely zero for two, or maybe zero for four when it came to interactions with her.

"Gabby!" Emi squealed. She held up a strawberry plant and waved. "I'm here!" As if Gabby wasn't standing two feet away from her. "And you're here too with us!"

Gabby's face softened immediately. And there it was, that warmth, that soft openness he'd been hoping to see again since that day at the pool before he'd been a cold jerk and wiped it from her face.

"We're worker bees. Me and Tessa Bear, at our new nursery. Want to see?"

Luca's smile widened at the nickname Emi had given her sister.

"Oh my, are you the cutest employees I've ever seen." The woman Gabby was with turned her smile on his girls and the twins beamed under her compliment. "I'm Mary. Who are you?"

"Mami"—Gabby paused, giving Luca a quick glance—"this is Tessa, Emilia and their dad, Luca. They just moved here from..."

"Boston," Luca said, extending his hand. "Nice to meet you, Mary."

"Mary is my mom." Gabby spoke to the girls, ignoring him.

He couldn't say why being so blatantly ignored made him smile. Perhaps because she was working so hard at it, right in front of him as if he couldn't see her. Didn't she have a clue? There was definitely something wrong with him that he took pleasure in her exerting so much energy not to notice him. He obviously hadn't been following her. Although, he'd gladly tag along like a needy puppy if she'd pay him one ounce of attention.

"You have a mom?" Tess whispered. She carefully climbed down from the wagon and went to stand right next to Gabby, taking her hand when she got close.

Please don't reject my daughter. The thought shot from his gut and lodged in his throat. The vise around his heart was a chokehold as he held his breath. But he needn't have worried. Gabby's whole demeanor calmed, and she squeezed Tess's hand, kneeling to get right at her level.

"I do...uh." She glanced at Luca with a question in her eyes.

But Emi beat him to the answer. "We don't."

His little lion looked so angry when she said it, it nearly threw Luca back a foot. They almost never talked about Noelle except in a wistful way, almost as if she were from a fairy tale they'd once read about. How could he have been so stupid? They were bound to have complicated emotions about it, about her.

All four pairs of female eyes pointed at him. The sun was up now, pointing at him too. Yep, it was definitely going to be a hot one. More people buzzed about the nursery. Conversations and laughter reached his ears. He took a deep breath of the morning air and his surroundings of watered plants and fresh dirt. The story wasn't pretty or easy, but he said the only thing he could in the situation, the words gritting in his throat. "She passed away a few years ago."

"We weren't even one year old yet." Emi stomped off the wagon and marched her way into Gabby's outstretched arm." Heartbreaking and funny at the same time. Luca crossed his arms and stifled the laugh that wanted to burst out of him. Even in absurd, awkward, sad situations, his lion was so dramatic. Luca had flashes of what it was going to be like with Emi as a teenager and he shuddered.

"No mom *and* we don't have lots of friends either, hardly any."

Luca coughed then and smacked his chest. Gabby shot wide eyes to him, both eyebrows raised, and he caught the smile she was trying to hide as well. Emi was her very own Dickens novel. It *was* sad, all of it and she was accurate on all accounts, but dammit she made him laugh.

"Well, what a perfect place you've moved to then," Mary said in her own dramatic voice about to embark on a grand tale.

Both his girls and Gabby gazed at her.

"I'm a mom and all my kids are grown. So you can visit me anytime. I have lots of love to shower, especially since I still don't have any grandchildren."

A flash of pain wrecked Gabby's face but she tilted it down so quickly and at the angle she knelt by his girls, with her sunhat, he could no longer see it.

"And Graciella is a special place, almost magical, some people say, with so many good people for making friends."

"Magical," his girls said in awe.

"I mean look at you already. Gabby's your friend. Now I'm your friend."

"Hey, girls! Want a popsicle?" Ana jogged toward them, her nursery apron tied around her waist. "The popsicle truck is here. Come see. Is it okay, Luca? I'll watch them."

He nodded. "Sure."

"Oh, I see Ana's your friend too," Mary said. She winked at the girls. "I think I'd like a popsicle. They have the best lemonade raspberry ones you've ever tasted." She gave Luca a smile, winked at him too, and whisked the twins away, leaving him standing alone with Gabby.

And he almost chuckled at Mary's mastery in maneuvering them into this situation. She was more than a mom. She was a wizard. And he would have thanked her for it if he hadn't felt the uncomfortable edge of tension stretching between him and Gabby in the wicked silence they now found themselves in.

"All right?" he asked, offering his hand. She was still kneeling on the cement.

"What? Oh." She closed her eyes and brought herself back to their space and he wanted to ask her where she'd disappeared to for a few seconds. What had happened to give her that ghostly paleness that washed over her face and left her eyes full of pain?

"I'm fine." She took his hand but removed it almost immediately once she was standing. The absence hit him acutely. As she stood, she'd brushed a tear from her cheek and the desire to comfort her surged through him.

"So you...uh...work here too?" She huffed and tossed her arm out toward the nursery. *Her defenses are up.* Shame, there was something about this woman, not that he didn't enjoy her attitude, but with each encounter, he wanted to peel it away and see what was underneath. "Sorry." She rubbed her eyes. "I'm being huffy for no reason. That was rude of me. And I'm so sorry about…um…about the girls' mom."

She stood by the table of strawberry plants, fidgeting with them. Luca picked up his pricing tool and continued putting stickers on the plants. He handed one to her and nodded toward the table and without hesitation, she was helping him arrange the strawberries while they talked.

"When I made the decision to move out here, I discovered the nursery was for sale. It was a sign, in a long line of many, that I was doing the right thing. A landscape business with its own nursery is a great combination. So I bought it."

"Nathan's Nursery? For Luca Rossi?" A tiny smile quirked her lips, but she quickly hid it.

"Well, it came with the name. The girls and I haven't decided on a new one yet. Their vote is for the Friendly Pink Unicorn."

Gabby laughed and Luca's nerves settled. "Let me guess, Pink was Emi's contribution, Friendly was Tess's and Unicorn was yours?"

He barked out a laugh then. Jesus her teasing felt good, even better when she did it while smiling at him. "You got the first two right. I told them we should think of plants and gardening when we rename it so people will have an idea what kind of shop it is. Any and all suggestions are welcome." He glanced at her. "So, you enjoy gardening?"

"I…uh…I do. I used to. It's been a while. My mom's a master gardener, but with a yard the size of my pinky.

She has some old favorites, but she also likes to change it up a bit in spring. I'm here to help her rein it in."

"Hmm." Luca glanced at Mary across the nursery, captivating his girls with a story he couldn't hear. They all had popsicles and Mary spoke as much with her hands as her voice. "She indulges you, huh?"

Gabby laughed, then caught herself. She studied him for a moment. "How could you tell?"

"Just a guess. But she seems pretty confident and sure of herself. I don't imagine she's a pushover."

"Hmm," Gabby said.

"Like mother like daughter, I'm guessing." She stared at him, no quick glances then skating away, but it was contemplative, and he sensed her mind drifting elsewhere. "Also, so you know, I don't mind you being huffy." That got a grin from her, and her shoulders relaxed a tiny bit. "Want to see some of the flowers I thought would fit your festival theme?"

"Sure," she said. "You…um…mentioned some calla lilies, pink ones. I don't think I've ever seen any but white."

"Over here." He hesitated, then led the way, ignoring the instinct that had him wanting to take her hand and gently nudge her along. Afraid that as soon as he turned his back, she'd dart away and disappear. But when he reached the perennials section, he was relieved to see she'd followed him. "They're still buds yet. You can barely see the pink. Here." He cut a stem and held it out to her, running his thumb over the coiled bud of the flower as she held it.

"Oh." Her joyful tone of surprise caught him off guard and sent a goofy grin across his face. "They're going to be perfect. And these ones here—wow, are they black?"

Luca cut a stem from the plant she pointed to and handed it to her. "The bud's blackish now, but when it opens it'll be a deep dark purple."

"How brilliant," she said with hushed awe.

"They're stunning," he replied, studying her. He swore she moved an inch closer. "Put them in a vase with water. They should bloom in a few days, maybe a week. Stubborn sometimes, calla lilies, but worth it."

"Really?" she asked.

"Absolutely."

"Gabriella, you didn't tell me you were working with Luca on the festival." Mary returned with his daughters, each hand of hers holding one of theirs, half-eaten popsicles held in their others.

"Oh, Lord." Gabby took a step back, his disappointment following her. He really was a sad, lonely stray, desperate for her attention.

"Emi, Tess and I have decided." Mary faced Luca. "You three are coming to dinner tonight. I hope five o'clock works. That way the girls can help me make cookies before dinner while you two work on your plan."

"Gabriella, huh?" He nudged her arm and she huffed.

"Pretty please, Daddy," his girls squealed. "We've never ever made cookies before."

Well now, that wasn't exactly true. He'd made cookies with them a time or two. Mostly probably rushing through the actions. Baking wasn't exactly his strong suit. One of his hopes in moving here was to be surrounded by friends, to give the girls a better life. And when he had a goal, he put one hundred percent effort into it. *Wouldn't hurt one bit to get to see Gabby again.* A broad smile filled his face. "We'd love to come." The offer to make cookies with Mary had put stars in their eyes and there was no way he'd deny them this. Plus—he beamed—spending more time with Gabriella Flores put stars in his.

Chapter Nine

"So, a man's coming to dinner?" Mary said in the car on the way home, like a teenage girl whose best friend just got asked out by a sexy musician at a concert.

"He's coming for you. You're the one who invited him." Gabby rolled down her window and let the warm air bathe her face. The air conditioning was too cold, too stifling, and she wanted to feel the breeze. Luca Rossi certainly made her *feel* when he looked at her. Correction, *into* her. As though he could turn every single button inside her on with that smile, the sexy flirty eyebrows, even his arms crossed over that fine chest of his.

And you want to let him, indulge him. Where had that thought come from?

"Ha." Her mom laughed. "Don't be ridiculous. He is coming for one reason and one reason only."

"To let his daughters make cookies with the town's most interfering know-it-all?"

"Oh, honey, you're cute when you pretend you don't know what's going on."

"I'm not pretending. I haven't pretended anything since...well, since you know who." Gabby pulled into their driveway and began helping her mom unload the nursery purchases into the yard. It was a few moments before Mary spoke.

"Now, maybe some mistakes were yours, Gabriella, but falling in love with a man wasn't one of them. You can't help what your heart decides to do. Unfortunately, that man was weak. His sins are his alone. Never take on the sins of someone else, honey, especially those of an asshole."

Gabby stared at her mom.

"What?" Mary asked. "You don't think I understand there are crappy people in the world because I've spent most of my life in a happy relationship in small-town Graciella?"

"No." Gabby shook her head. "It's not that. I don't think I've ever heard you swear before."

"Hmm, well, no one ever tried to harm my child. Unless you count that puny jerk Marissa in middle school who cheated off Cammy's work and tried to blame Cammy."

Gabby's anger at herself melted away until only the dregs remained. They worked in silence for a few moments, Gabby trying to gather her thoughts and her mother letting her. It was how the two of them had always worked together.

"I'm...it's hard to trust again, myself mostly," she said quietly.

"You can't keep punishing yourself, honey. I know it doesn't disappear easily, but be here, in the now, and move forward. Learn from it and keep going. But learn the right lessons. That's all you can do," Mary said. "I do know a thing or two about relationships blowing up and moving forward."

Gabby smiled. If only her blown-apart life could end as well as her mother's had.

"He's very easy to look at."

"Yes." Gabby sighed. "Luca Rossi is very easy on the eyes." He really was, even, or maybe especially, in his sweaty T-shirt, those long legs of his tapering off into his running shoes. His special deep blue eyes that memorized her with their concentration.

"Oooo and the way he was gazing at you. I was surprised his tongue wasn't hanging out drooling." That got a laugh out of Gabby. "Magic in those eyes, let me tell you."

Gabby studied her mom, so observant, always talking about magic. Gabby wasn't sure she believed in such things anymore. "I'm going to run a few errands. Text me a list if you need anything for tonight."

* * * *

She went to the one place she trusted above all else, save her family — the shore. Carefully she navigated the steep winding trail down to the hidden beach. It wasn't really hidden, but most people ignored it because it was more difficult to access. Gabby loved this quiet part of Graciella, the solitude. There was something about kicking off her sandals and walking barefoot across the wet beach, the wide ribbon of sand stretching out ahead of her. Soft white edges of foam remained from where the waves had gently pushed onto shore.

Following the wave's path for a while, she finally turned and faced the ocean, deep tealy blue bleeding into a light blue sky. It was the sea she needed now, more than anything. So many things she'd lost or tried to change over the last two years, to fit someone else's idea of beauty. Her feet hit the water and she kept walking up to her knees, baggy pants rolled up, but not nearly far enough.

She wanted to go deeper, but she didn't have her swimsuit with her. She tugged her pants higher and let the water splash and play against her shins. Johnny had always commented on her legs, how big they were, how *"They were okay if you liked that sort of thing, or if you weren't from L.A."*

So she'd started hiding her legs, wearing long dresses and flowy skirts that skimmed her ankles. She used to love her legs. They were long and muscular. She'd once considered them powerful. Then she'd let an idiot crawl into her thoughts and make her self-conscious about them. *About so many things.*

Gabby ran and splashed through the water, like a child learning how to swim for the first time. Like Emi and Tess in all their wonder. That was what she wanted to regain, and she was determined to, racing out her anger and doubt.

When her lungs burned, she slowed and took deep breaths of the salty sea air, clean and briny. It cleansed her throat along with her thoughts. Standing still, she watched the sunlight glint off the low, lazy waves. As the water moved into her and pushed against the shore, she stood still and studied the blue depths. They'd never lied to her. They never lied at all.

Now they were mostly calm, the shimmery surface meandering in a lazy sunny path. Sometimes the water was so still, glasslike, mirroring everything. During a storm, waves raced and rushed, a churning fury underneath, dangerous to anyone in their path, but still true. Never any games, or manipulations. What she saw was what she got, if she was smart enough to learn, to pay attention, to trust. *Exactly like Luca's eyes.*

But how could she know that about him already? The man intrigued her, against her better judgment, especially since she'd sworn off men. That shield didn't seem to work when it came to him. So, what did she want to do about it, if anything? That question flitted through her mind and danced across her skin.

Gabby left the shore both rejuvenated and contemplative, and as she wove through the streets of Graciella, she paid attention to every little thing, new and old. When she was home and showered, she filtered through her closet for something to wear that said, what? *Interested, maybe. Oh, shit.* Was she interested? *Yes, no, absolutely not, maybe?* Her emotions were so erratic.

Now was not the time to focus on a man. Now was the time to reclaim herself. Gabby laughed away her ridiculousness and confusion. There was one dress that kept catching her eye, one of the long ones she'd purchased in California. She'd loved it for the color. But she'd never worn it because the deep fuchsia was too bright for every event they'd been going to attend, Johnny had said.

Hmm. Gabby took it off the hanger and held it to her body. Then she smiled huge for the first time in maybe two years as an idea took shape. She dragged out her sewing machine and scissors and got busy cutting off inches of the fabric and sewing a new hem, one that would show off her amazing legs and make her feel good about herself, for herself, not for any man at all.

Chapter Ten

Mary's house was on a quiet street not too far from downtown on a block with old cottages, each one different and charming in its own way. Gabby wasn't kidding when she said her mom's yard was tiny. Mary had crammed the flowers in, but everything belonged and looked gorgeous together. Luca also wondered if her plants were on steroids. As they walked to the door, he even noticed some plants he'd never seen before. Huh, maybe she'd come work for him too.

"Oh, aren't you delightful. You must be Emi, Tess and Luca. I'm Isa. Come on in." A tall woman with straight white hair cut in a sleek bob around her head opened the door to them. She was wearing a black jumpsuit and wedge heels with a line of thin bracelets up one arm. Blue eyes, striking against her brown skin and a smile that lit her entire face—she could easily have graced a fashion runway in Milan.

"You made it." Gabby walked up next to Isa, linking their arms together, studying him.

"Are my cookie helpers here?" Mary called from somewhere in the house.

"Did you meet Isa?" Gabby asked. "Isa is my other mom."

There was a split second of silence before Emi stepped into Gabby and Isa's space, put her chubby little hands on her waist and said, "You have *two* moms?"

"I do." She beamed at his daughter.

"So, double the awesome," Luca said and held his hand out to Isa, who put one hand in his and her other on their clasped hands, with a comforting touch. But it was the tender smile on Gabby's face in that instant that made this whole evening worth it. Hell, it made his move across the country worth it.

"Two moms *and* a pretty dress." Emi looked at Luca. "Gabby is the luckiest person I've ever met."

"Wow," Tess whispered in awe. She put her hand out for Isa to shake too, his gem, processing everything before her. Then she went to Gabby and leaned into her side. That knot tightened in his chest at how comfortable his girls already were with Gabby. She fit into a spot that had been empty for so long. There was a moment when he worried he shouldn't let them get too close, but they'd already fallen half in love with her. Even though they were only four, he wanted them to be brave in love. And wasn't that a thought he'd have to think about when it came to himself. He felt completely off balance.

"I...did you..." Tess stumbled over her words, staring at Luca for help. Once again, Gabby beat him to it as she got down at Tess's level.

"What's that, honey?"

"Did you...um...miss not having a dad?" Tess whispered.

Gabby pulled both his daughters in and wiggled her eyebrows as if she had the most delicious secret to share. "Well, I actually have a great dad too, like you." She snuck a glance at Luca. "My parents divorced when I was little, but he lives in Graciella. So I have triple the awesome!"

"And that is a great reason to celebrate by making cookies." Mary swept in then, gave Luca a kiss on the cheek like he was part of the family, and she and Isa led the girls to the kitchen, leaving him and Gabby together.

"Gabriella," he said, taking pleasure in the barely repressed eye roll and smirk she gave him, as though he was teasing her by using her full name. When really, her name sounded sexy as hell on his lips. He was standing near enough to see the blush darken her cheeks too. "You look lovely." She might not be dating right now, but he could still be a gentleman. And damn, but he wanted to date her. Suddenly he wanted nothing more than to convince her to put so much more than dating on the table.

"It's pink." She wore a simple short sundress in a deep rosy color, almost red that showed off her long smooth legs, from her strong thighs all the way to some gold sandals. Her toenails matched her dress. He wanted to kneel at her feet and inspect them, see what kind of flower she'd painted on them this time. Luca gripped the wine bottle he was holding to keep from reaching for her. This need to fuse her body to his was growing inside him. He was desperate to caress her cheek, feel the heat and softness there.

Fingering the sides of her dress and giving a little sway, she said, "I...uh thought the...girls might appreciate it."

Is she flirting with me? Had it been that long that he didn't recognize it anymore, or was he uncertain because of the way she'd reacted the other night when he'd invited her for a drink? There was one way to find out.

"The girls?" he asked. "They obviously love it. So do I. The color suits you. Shows off your gorgeous legs." He took a step closer. "Bold and pretty."

Her eyes weren't shuttered or angry or annoyed, he took note. The gold in them sparkled. "Thank you," she whispered.

"You're welcome, Gabriella." This time there was no annoyance. In fact, he swore she leaned toward him, before quickly blinking and stepping away. She stood straight, smoothing down her dress, worry flashing across her expression.

Taking a clue from her uncomfortableness, he cleared his throat and handed her the wine. "For your moms. I was going to bring a plant from the nursery, but I thought I'd scope out Mary's garden first to see what she might need help with. I think she could teach me a few things. Her tulips are gigantic."

"Yeah," she said, her voice tender with love. "Some special ingredient in her compost, she claims. Although she swears never to tell anyone what it is, says it's the magical Graciella touch. She sprinkles her dust on every plant and they thrive for her."

I bet you have your own magic. And he was aching to discover it.

"Come on out to the patio. Isa made her signature painkillers if you want a cocktail."

All sense of tension was gone, and she gave him her soft smile, which was a million times better than her worry and whatever that had been that night he'd asked her to get a drink. He didn't ever want to put that expression on her face again. He already liked this woman, but there were layers to her that ran deep and maybe wounded. If he wanted anything with her, even simply friendship, he needed to tread very carefully. *I want more than friendship.*

Luca happily followed her. "I have no idea what a painkiller is, but I'm game."

"They're delicious if you're into rum and coconut. Makes you believe you're on vacation on some balmy tropical island."

"Ah, well in that case, yes, please." Luca had his notebook with him. "I added some structural lines to your original sketch. What do you think?"

They sat at the outdoor table. It was set with a pitcher of water, a pitcher of a frothy cocktail, some snacks and small napkins. The tiny but lush backyard surrounded them. An oasis in the middle of a neighborhood. The sound of a fountain added to the serenity. Luca made a mental note to amp up the fountain section of the nursery. He couldn't make out the expression on Gabby's face as she pondered his additions to her drawings. *Damn, she's good at camouflage.*

"This is amazing."

Ahh, there she is, not hiding, just processing everything then offering her thoughts.

"It's like you superimposed my ideas on an architectural drawing, and it...it's oddly wonderful together. Where did you learn to draw so beautifully?"

"I've been an architect for fifteen years. It's what I left in Boston."

"That's a long time." She studied him. "Was it, uh, difficult to leave the place? I mean was that where your…um, wife died?"

"We weren't married. I…" Damn, it was still a painful subject, although, Luca thought, it had lessened over the years. The pain came more from the reminder that he'd failed Noelle and his girls. "It's…it's not a happy story," he said. And the last thing he wanted to talk about with a pretty woman on a lush spring evening.

"I shouldn't have pried." She poured them both water and a cocktail, a flush climbing up her neck as she avoided eye contact with him.

Inwardly Luca flinched. He didn't want to make her feel bad for having asked either. "No. It's that most people don't really want to hear it after they've actually heard it, if that makes sense. Once the reality hits them."

He never spoke about it to anyone, except his own mother. And even then it was uncomfortable times one thousand. His mother had a hard time talking about most serious things after they lost Dom. Even now she spent her time floating from one cruise adventure to another, only stepping foot back in reality a few times a year to see the girls.

"I…" She took a deep breath. "I don't mind listening."

He'd hoped for an opening with her, and this was absolutely the last angle he'd expected. Maybe she didn't date—maybe she'd only ever want to be friends. Being vulnerable had never been his strong suit, certainly not as a young man when he'd lost his brother. When Noelle died, he shut himself off to anything vulnerable or risky.

"*You need change*," he'd told himself back in November, mired in the fog of his life. He'd just finished listening to a meditation app about vulnerability. It had stuck with him like a punch to the gut. That as much as being vulnerable left you open to getting hurt, it also opened the doors for meaningful connection. "*Big change, all of you, not just the girls.*"

He'd been dragging through life one responsibility at a time, not enjoying any of it. Cranky with the girls, exhausted, without connection to anyone. Closing himself off hadn't been good for him or his daughters. Unfortunately, he didn't feel very skilled in how to change that. Luca made the decision to share before he could toss it around any longer.

"Noelle was her name. I met her at work. We were together for almost five years before she got pregnant. It was unexpected." Luca swallowed and as much as he wanted to look away, race through the rest, Gabby held his gaze. "After the initial shock, she…we both wanted the girls, but neither of us realized how hard it was going to be. She got very depressed after they were born. We were both exhausted, trying to work and be new parents and I…I missed so many signs. She took some pills one afternoon. I…I found her when I came home from work, on the floor. The girls were asleep in their crib."

"Luca," Gabby whispered. She wiped a tear from her cheek and unexpectedly placed her hand on his.

He found his own cheeks wet. He grabbed one of the napkins and wiped his face. "Sorry. It's…um…it's been a long time. I never…we don't talk about it, that part."

"Please don't apologize."

"It's no excuse, but it's why I was a complete jerk that first day we saw you. You were on the floor, and it all came rushing back to me. I think I had a sort of anxiety attack, barely kept it together really until we made it into the air conditioning in the ice cream place, and I could sit for a while." Luca took his glass of water and chugged it. "I don't think I ever realized how angry I still am at her until I saw you on the floor. It doesn't make any sense, I know."

"That's a tragedy for you and your girls. And I don't think you owe anyone any explanation about your feelings. I'm sorry for ruining the evening, making you expose your pain."

He shook his head. "It helps to talk about it. I hadn't realized how much." The evening was so quiet. Anyone gazing out at them would see two people having a casual conversation with cocktails. Meanwhile, his heart beat a mile a minute and he wondered if he should be the one to run and hide this time. The tiny squeeze of her hand on his had his heart begging for more.

"Hey," he said, tugging gently on her hand. "It's still a great evening, in my opinion."

Chapter Eleven

"Mm." Gabby smiled. What should she say? That she agreed? She did. She hadn't felt this comfortable and free or close to someone in a while, but she was so afraid, so cautious. He'd shared his tragedy with her. *"Helps to talk about it."* Lily had said something similar. The words he'd offered her chipped away at her walls. There was such heartbreak and sadness and grief, but it was all, his honesty especially, somehow exactly what she'd needed.

He huffed out a breath and took a sip of his cocktail. "That's tasty. Painkiller, huh? Fitting name after that conversation." He tipped his drink to hers. "Cheers."

She laughed and clinked glasses. Maybe they were all a mess, but maybe figuring out how to wade through the mess and live anyway was what strengthened them. When she'd left L.A., her emotions singed raw, she hadn't been sure she wanted to be stronger, *could* be. Now, sitting next to a man who'd endured some of the worst heartbreak she could imagine, his willingness to share with her, had her wondering if her own strength was simply waiting for her to embrace it.

"We get to have that drink together after all, huh?" he said.

Ugh. She wrapped her lips around her straw and let the cold coconut and pineapple soothe her parched mouth. Her brain still insisted she shouldn't want a relationship right now, absolutely couldn't handle the implosion of falling for someone only to be cut down again. But she couldn't help the disappointment that he'd only asked her out to talk about the festival.

"For what it's worth," he said quietly. "I *was* asking you out that evening, because I wanted to spend time with you, Gabriella."

She met his gaze with surprise. *Is he a mind reader too?* He still held her hand in his. She studied their entwined fingers, both long and defined, her darker skin and bright rosy nail polish against his tan skin and short blunt nails. She wanted to run her fingers over his, inspect each one, sketch them in different poses, listen to what they had to say, see if she could learn more about this man simply by studying his hardworking hands.

"I don't want to make you uncomfortable." He grinned and it caressed her nerves. The blue of his eyes had changed as the sunlight faded, their aqua deep and…and, if she could only get closer, she could see if they really were swirled with hints of silver and green. "But tell me if it's not what you want. Are you…are you interested in my…advances?"

Oh, wow. What…how did she answer? "Advances, huh?" She teased to avoid the pounding of her nerves and was rewarded with his sexy smile and another tug on her hand. It was both a struggle and exhilarating to be caught in his gaze. And something more, something grounding. She'd noticed it the first time she saw him. She'd have to unpack that later when she was alone. What did he mean by advances anyway? A busy single dad with two little girls and a new, or rather two new businesses. *Does he mean something easy and physical, a spring fling?* Maybe she could do that, enjoy some *advances* from a sexy man. *Casual, fun, flirty.* "I think I might be."

"You think, huh?" *Oh no. Is that disappointment flashing across his face?* What just happened? Was he disappointed because she'd said yes? *I'm so confused.*

"Gabby, honey," Isa yelled from the sliding door. "Can you grab your big platter for my salad, the pretty green one? Oh, you should show Luca your apartment while you're at it. We girls are in here having a lovely time without you."

"*Madre de dios,*" she muttered, and Luca laughed.

"Bold and stubborn, but not subtle, are they?" he asked.

"Never subtle, no." She'd always thought that a wonderful thing to be raised by two outgoing, bold women, along with her father. She'd been bold and fun once too. Jesus, she'd shoved away so much of herself she'd practically forgotten how to flirt. "Well, Luca Rossi, you better follow me if you don't want to disappoint my mothers."

"I definitely don't want that." He chuckled. She fidgeted with her hands, not knowing what to do with them now that she wasn't tethered to him. She'd gone from not liking the man to being mildly annoyed by him to infatuation in a matter of days. And she certainly didn't understand that.

"Wow. This is…" Luca crossed his arms and studied her small one-bedroom apartment. Normally her vaulted ceilings made the place seem large, but with him in her space, standing there so contemplative and serious, everything felt crowded, pushing in on her.

Here he was in her solitude, her safety, her beautiful home. It wasn't too messy, but she had clutter here and there, scarves draped over the windows, vases full of dried flowers, one with fresh. Books littered her coffee table and her small kitchen island. She never seemed to have enough bookcases.

"I was going to say not at all what I expected, but I…you." He ran his hand over her plush green velvet sofa, and along the deep dark pink walls. He eyed her tall bookcases as if he could figure her out by what books she owned. He stopped in front of her bright and colorful abstract painting of two bodies embracing, linked together in passion, an explosion of bold beauty.

"What do you think?" she blurted. She didn't want to know. She did. She wanted to hide under her covers when he offered his thoughts. Gabby was so intimately tied to her home. Her emotions were everywhere on every surface. And right now, they fluttered under her skin in anticipation.

"This is you," he said in his rich voice.

Oh. Her heart peeked out from its hiding place.

"The real you, not the one who's hiding."

How does he know? She tried to take slow deep breaths without him noticing.

"Gabriella?"

She snapped her eyes open. From across the room, he stared at her, sending out a link connecting them. The vibration of it seeped into her skin, dug under her ribs and warmed her blood. *I don't know whether to step nearer or back away.* Her pulse hummed as he took the decision out of her hands. Finally closing the vast canyon between them, he crossed to her.

"Can I touch you?"

"Yes." She nodded in case he couldn't hear her over the hum coming from her body. He didn't take her hand, but standing before her, so close, she found it difficult to breathe as he stroked his fingers up her arm and brushed his thumb over her bare shoulder.

"I knew it would be soft." He toyed with the thin strap of her dress, concentrating on that one tiny strip of fabric that stood between him and all of her, and sent erotic shivers through her. His other hand did the same, trailed along her arm to the strap of her dress. Then he slowly brought his hands around her back and urged her to him. It was as if he spoke and her body obeyed.

She leaned in, her worries and anticipation coalescing into want. The heat of his hands on her skin was so lovely that she wished she was naked. Nothing, not one thing between them so she could feel what his hands did to her bare skin. He leaned in and whispered against her ear, "Gabriella?" and she shuddered.

"Huh?" Her head fell to the side in offering. Would it be bad if she held him there, begged him to kiss her exactly where her pulse threatened to slam right out of her skin?

"I want to kiss you." He breathed in. She didn't know which was making her wetter, his mouth grazing her sensitive skin or his breath trailing after it. His knees nearly gave out and she gripped his shoulders to keep from falling.

"Uh-huh." She was dizzy with want. *Yes, please kiss me.*

His hands moved to her waist. The warmth of his touch soothed and delighted. "But earlier..." His voice was a caress.

"Earlier?" She let out a breath, more like a pant, an animal in heat.

"When I asked about my advances." His lips hovered by her ear now. "You said, '*I think.*'"

What? She was dizzy now with desire. Her nipples were hard and pressing against him. She wondered if he could feel it, wanted him to, wanted him to put those powerful hands of his on her right there.

He put an inch of space between them. "You don't seem certain, and I want you to be sure. One hundred percent sure."

She closed her eyes, but he could still see her. There really was no hiding with this man. He linked their hands again, both of his in both of hers. "I'm...I was with someone," she blurted. Air huffed out of her, embarrassment, distaste. "Not recently...or...well, I mean, I...it's been almost eight months since he broke..." *Broke me.* "Cheated on me."

He didn't let go and she could have wept at how much that meant to her. "Christ, Gabby. I'm sorry, that's awful."

"It's not...it is..." She shook her head. "I mean it's not in the way you think. I...it turns out it wasn't a good relationship. It's embarrassing how far it was from what I thought, what I dreamt, what I deserved."

"Hey." Luca squeezed her hands. Thank God he was holding on. Her emotions were spinning out of control, her tears ready to explode. "Gabby, look at me."

She opened her eyes and his were full of concern. "Are you okay?"

"I don't know." They spilled over then, not a damn bursting as she'd expected, more fluidly, a letting go. "I'm getting there. Seems like an extremely slow climb. Some moments I'm not great…things come rushing in. But since I came home, I've been trying to find myself again." *Alone.*

He gave her an intimate smile she swore she could feel between her legs, used his gorgeous thumbs to wipe her tears and wrapped her in his warm arms. It was the last thing she expected, and again, exactly what she needed. "Something happens to me in your presence. All these…sensations…I…"

"I feel it too," he said. "And I like the you I've seen so far. I'd like to get to know more of you."

"Okay." It was all she was capable of as she held on and let his strength bleed into her. She could do this, show him a little more, show him the parts of her that wouldn't scare him away, keep it light and casual. "Maybe you could be patient with me, and I'll be honest with you about how I'm feeling."

"Yeah." He smiled and brushed his fingers along her cheek and under her lip. "That sounds good."

"'Kay." Gabby leaned into his touch, her lips a breath away from his. She felt like purring against him. Maybe she was.

"I'm going to need to work on my patience," he said. His voice had dipped low and husky. He gripped her hips and set her gently away from him.

Gabby didn't want him to. She wanted to strip it away and see what happened, *feel* what happened. But it felt soft and fluttery to be with someone who took care with her, with everything she'd said. And that was too wonderful to shove aside.

"What do you say we find that platter and go enjoy dinner?"

"Sure." Gabby used her restroom to take a few deep breaths and fix her makeup. She found the pretty botanical plate Isa was talking about and strolled back to the house hand in hand with Luca.

"Think I'll get in trouble?" He plucked a magnolia blossom from their tree and gently fitted it behind her ear, trailing his fingers along her jaw when he was finished. "We'll pretend it was on the ground." He winked at her and took her hand in his again.

"Okay," she said and pretended she wasn't inwardly freaking out that her heart had just exploded from the tiniest bit of attention from Luca Rossi on a pretty evening in April with some of her scars on full display.

Chapter Twelve

"Are you sure we can fit them all?" Gabby stood in the middle of Main Street with Lily early on Tuesday morning, *early* early. Too early for someone who wasn't a morning person herself and who had been pulling too many all-nighters racing against her salon opening clock.

She took a pull of the latte Lily had brought her. Lily had enough energy for both of them and had arrived with coffee and croissants. *Best friends and morning bakeries with mouthwatering pastries should get gold medals.* It was three weeks until the festival, and time was whooshing by. Thank goodness she wasn't the main person in charge of the entire event, because her salon opening was fast approaching as well.

"You doubt me?" Lily scoffed. Her confidence alone could get things done.

Gabby scanned the list of festival vendors. Twenty farm and craft retail booths. Ten booths of games and activities and of course a face painting station for the kids. In the very middle, they'd have a tiny stage for different musical guests throughout the day. "Never. But even you can't make the street bigger or longer." There was only so much Main Street to be used. "We haven't accounted for the food booths." Gabby couldn't wait for the tamale booth and the elephant ears. She was definitely having both at the festival, maybe even some firecracker popcorn too.

"You're right. Dammit," Lily said. "How could I forget the food? What is wrong with me? Do I have a fever?"

Gabby felt Lily's forehead. "You do feel flushed. But can we revisit the part about me being right?"

Lily's mouth dropped open.

"What?" Gabby asked.

"I think I had a glimpse of my confident badass friend Gabby Flores."

"Oh shush." She gave Lily a gentle shove but couldn't help smiling. She hoped Lily was right. She was finding her spark, little by little. On Sunday morning after another quiet walk on the shore, she'd stopped at the Art Attic and picked out a new sketchbook, a set of colored pencils and some gorgeous thin markers. The book was silver and sparkly with a bold red poppy on it. It was time for a fresh start and Sunday she'd decided to uncover her sparkle.

She was wasting time being annoyed by what she'd lost or sacrificed in Los Angeles, forcing herself to exist in some sterile image. An image that Johnny had planted in her thoughts. *A weed.* Nope, it was time to begin again. She was giddy at the thought. A person really could have a fresh start.

She'd decorated the beginning pages with bright images, flowers, mermaids, doodles in deep hues of every color, with no specific design in mind. It had been freeing. Slowly, after that, with much concentration, she'd drawn some additions to her salon that would take it from sterile to...well...to *her*. Pops of color and lush comfort, beauty splashed here and there.

Then she'd met her sister Cammy and her two employees and worked at her salon scrubbing corners and opening supplies, letting the mundane tasks work their meditation on her mind. Imagining had never been so exhilarating. Every time a new idea had popped up, she'd sketched the vision. Her salon, her dream could still be sophisticated without being boring, and Gabby Flores had never been boring. What in the heck had she been thinking?

It hadn't hurt that Luca had sent her sweet texts throughout the day. She'd woken Sunday to the first one.

Luca: Morning, Gabriella. Had a great time last night. Thank your moms for me for dinner again.

When she'd been eating lunch, he'd sent a precious picture of the girls having a picnic outside on a blanket with their stuffed animals.

Luca: The elephant is Mary, the owl is Isa and the unicorn is Gabby, according to Emi and Tess.

Later when the sun was high and hot and she was sweating while scrubbing around the outside window sills.

Luca: I'm having dreams about that dress you had on. About you in that dress. About what was underneath.

Whew, that one had been anything but sweet. She'd texted him back with simple emojis because she was at a loss for words each time. It would have been ridiculous to text "Swoon," each time. And she was really trying hard not to be ridiculous.

Last night she'd tucked herself into her soft couch with a glass of wine and she'd sketched a pair of hands, angular and strong with the power to arouse and comfort. *Luca's hands.* She'd drawn his face, those sexy lips of his parted in a knowing smile. The one he'd given her when he'd tucked the flower behind her ear in the garden at dusk. She'd filled in his sensual deep blue eyes, tried to capture the focus he aimed her way, the sense his eyes gave her that she was someone special.

"Ladies." And there he stood in the flesh. His voice vibrated across her skin. *Mm,* it was a shiver of delight racing through her. He'd turned her on with one tiny word. And his smile? It was no polite smile or cute grin, but full-on, megawatt *I want to kiss you* bravado. She could draw his face a million times, bent in full concentration toward her, the sexy laugh lines around his mouth, and never really capture how his heated smile felt in the moment. Damn, she could stare at that mouth all day.

She hadn't seen him since Saturday, since their…well, what did one call it? Embrace? Flirting session in her apartment where he'd nearly incinerated her panties with his voice and his touch, and…where she'd cried in his arms? *Good job, Gabriella. Oh well. He didn't seem to mind.* But maybe she'd needed some space, and maybe he'd sensed that, and had given it to her, while still staying connected with his texts.

Confident but patient, who knew that could be such a turn-on?

"Uh, wow!" Lily whispered and nudged Gabby out of her lust-hazed stupor. She gave Gabby a look that was a complete sentence. One only two best friends who'd grown up together could understand. It said, *"Oh, boy do we have a lot to talk about."*

"Hi, Luca," Gabby said, feeling that pull between them as if there was no one else in the universe but the two of them. And there was more awkward silence as they stared at each other.

"Uh, so..." Lily took a loud slurp of her smoothie, interrupting the sparkly stare-down. "The planters are amazing, Luca. We were trying to figure out where the food booths should go." Lily showed him the plans.

Gabby ogled him as he grew serious. He was intense in such a sexy way. Confident in his body, not peacocky. Yet the show was so nice to look at.

"I had a thought about that. What if we continued the booths into this side alley here? It dead ends into the open steps that climb up the hill to Carriage Park."

Gabby tossed her empty coffee cup in the trash and followed Luca and Lily down the small alley, more like a wide unused section of the street that bordered her corner salon.

"I'd forgotten about this tiny hidden refuge. This area has never been much except an avenue to the steps," Lily contemplated out loud. "And look at them now, overtaken with vines."

"I'll clean it up, reveal the steps and the nice grassy area at the bottom. We could have the food booths here, maybe move your musicians this way too, or not, if you wanted to keep it more relaxed. Set out some tables and chairs. People could also use the grass and extra steps for seating. It'll have sun and shade during the festival, and it wouldn't impact any more traffic or parking." He spoke with his hands and Gabby pictured it.

"I see the potential. You made it come to life, Luca," Lily said.

Good thing her friend could talk. Gabby's words were a tangle in her throat. Maybe because she was too busy being overwhelmed by his body, the way he moved, all sensual long limbs so in tune with the world around him. *I bet he's gorgeous when he swims, snaking in and out of the water, smooth and sleek and strong.*

"And I can see how having a calm place would be nice for people if they're overwhelmed in the crowds, or they need a rest," Lily said.

"I can build a few more planters and we can add garlands and lights above the music area and steps to bring it together."

Bring us together. All your graceful limbs tangled up in me. Gabby shivered at the thought.

"Perfect." Lily sucked down the rest of her drink, the slurping noise an intrusion into Gabby's fantasy.

"Thirsty much?" Gabby teased.

Lily gazed at the empty cup as though she had no idea where the drink had gone. "I need to go, you two. I have meetings this morning and it's imperative I get another lemonade smoothie to tide me over."

"Be careful. You might turn into one of those if you're not careful."

Lily laughed. "I can't get enough of them lately. They're so tart, with a hint of sweet. I crave them all the time. I'll...uh...see you two later." She walked away muttering to herself.

"Pretty morning." Luca was right by her side." It was only the two of them now. Gabby pressed her back against the brick of the building to find purchase as her emotions swirled around her.

"Where...where are the girls?"

"Preschool." Luca took her hand and twined their fingers together and something settled inside her at the same time as her heart swooned.

"This...uh...this early?" she stuttered as he ran his thumb across her fingers.

"The Learning Center has early drop-offs, but considering they're awake before the sun, this is practically mid-day for them."

"Mm." She smiled. "They're morning people. I bet you are too. I should have known." She rolled her eyes with the tease.

Luca chuckled and nudged his body closer. "You're not?"

"Absolutely not." She shuddered.

"I love the early mornings."

His voice had gone husky. Oh wow, how sexy he was when he spoke low and needy. Was that how she affected him?

"When everyone and everything hasn't woken up yet. Quiet, full of potential. If you're really lucky, you might see a brilliant colorful sunrise." His hand smoothed over her cheek and behind her neck, cupping her there, holding her head preciously in his very competent hand, his thumb teasing along her ear, so soft it flirted between a caress and a tickle and had every cell in her body standing at attention.

"Hmm." She purred again as he leaned in. There was no other word for it. He brushed her lips with his thumb, followed the movement with his gaze, directing the electricity skimming through her blood. Then he aimed those gorgeous eyes right at hers.

"Kiss me," she whispered and grabbed onto his hand, feeling the pulse on his wrist throbbing under his skin. When she spoke, she got to see the smile light his eyes.

"You sure?"

"Oh yes." She nodded as if the words weren't enough on their own.

Fitting his other hand to her back, Luca gently pulled them flush against each other. She could feel his body everywhere next to hers. *And he hasn't even kissed me yet.* Her mind was still cautious, but her body had other ideas. Barely restraining from wrapping her leg around him right here in this glorious early morning, out in the open for anyone to see, Gabby leaned up the last inch and brushed her lips to his. Her eyes fluttered at the soft contact.

For a second, they explored each other tentatively, soft lips, warmth unfurling around them, weaving a spell. Luca groaned and tugged her to him, really to him this time. There was no mistaking how he felt, how every last inch of him felt. He tipped her head and took her mouth like he was possessed. He tasted like mint and sunshine. And she wrapped her hands around his head and held on.

She made a sound that was not of her body, or at least not in her life so far. And he ripped his away from her.

"Damn," he swore. "Meant to take you out on a date first. A classy woman deserves some classy attention. Some dancing, walking hand in hand in the moonlight, delicious meals…"

His eyes were fixed on her mouth as he rubbed her bottom lip with that thumb of his that sent shivers right to her pussy. Her imagination was in overdrive. *Whoa.*

She set her heels on solid ground and he took a small step back. The soft summer air flitted between them, making her ache to be plastered against him again.

This was so different from anyone she'd ever been with — her body's one-hundred-percent physical awareness of his, her mind's synching with his, her heart beating out of control. She hummed with an intimacy she'd never encountered before. Everything else around her washed away in a blur. Her only focus was his face and the intensity in his eyes and, for everything that was magical, the sweep of his fingers against her electrified skin.

"Got carried away," he said and cleared his throat. "Been a long time since that's happened. So long it feels like the first. First kiss, *best* kiss I've ever had."

Oh, damn. He was killing her. She sighed into him, and he wrapped his arms around her. It felt so good. No one, absolutely no one had ever hugged her the way he did, with desire and protection at the same time. Or kissed her that way. Her body was still lit.

But am I seeing something meaningful as I did with John? Only to be the fool once more? She'd been caught in John's spell in the beginning. Or had she? He'd had an air of Hollywood about him, the glamour and stars. That was what she'd been caught up in. Luca was everything different, grounded, strong, focused.

She pulled out of Luca's arms. He stepped off the curb so she was slightly taller than him. Holding her hand in his, he stroked her fingers, jarring her out of memories and right here to this moment. She wanted to climb right back into him, have him surround her with his arms, stroke her whole body the way he did her fingers.

"Want to go out on a date with me, Gabriella? Saturday night? You could wear one of those sexy dresses and I could fantasize about you the whole night?"

"A date with you sounds lovely, but Saturday is my opening. We're having a cocktail celebration at five that evening, here. You could…uh…come." He made asking her out on a date look so easy, and yet inviting him to her opening was anything but. Her neck heated with embarrassment. Maybe she shouldn't have asked him. Did one do that for a casual relationship?

"I'd love to come."

Simple words and her flush of anxiety burst into happiness.

"You remind me of a sunrise, Gabriella." His voice had dipped low and husky again as he directed all his beauty her way.

"I do?" she whispered. *What is he talking about?* He could say anything to her right now with that stroke of his thumb and she'd follow along.

"Each hint of color another layer to discover. First lavender, streaks of orange and peach seeping into bright pink. Until the sun is fully visible over the horizon, then…" His voice was its own caress.

"Then?"

"Then…" He cupped her cheek. "The day is fully formed right before your eyes and there's this beautiful bright star, shining her brilliance on you. Infusing the whole world with color." He kissed her palm. "Have a good day, Gabriella." As if he hadn't just lit a burst of fireworks around her heart.

She watched him walk away, climb into his truck and drive off in the low haze of the morning. The world around her slowly returned to her senses. Two crows cawed their annoyance on the corner. Soft air filtered through the new pale green leaves of the birch trees. The fresh scent of the sun warmed the land. A produce van drove down Main.

Anyone could have seen her practically mauling Luca, climbing him. Had she climbed him? Or had that been a fantasy? She'd never gotten so lost in a haze of desire before. Her body still felt boneless. But it wasn't really her body she was most concerned with, or even anyone seeing her.

She'd just invited him to her salon opening party. The most important night in her life so far. Standing with the building propping her up, the stable safe foundation she'd built for herself since returning exploded into dust. It was her heart she feared for now, a trapped bird beneath her ribs, wanting to risk everything and take flight.

Chapter Thirteen

Gabby had yet to visit Brockman Farms since she'd returned. The new café and addition hadn't been finished when she'd left. *It looks amazing!* Although it was attached to the main house, it was wholly new and unique stretching out to the side, like a goddess opening her arms to the sky in freedom and delight. Tall floor-to-ceiling windows had the sun's rays bouncing off the glass to make rainbows on the freshly mowed lawn.

An inviting double-door entrance with antique doors had a touch of old Parisian style. A covered side patio offered a lovely spot for al fresco dining. She saw the lights draped across the top and could picture the pretty setting at night, glowing and glimmering and highlighting those glass panels as well. It was, in a word, fabulous. Grand without being ostentatious, especially with the hanging flower planters and fun mismatched chairs.

Lily had invited her this morning before it opened for the day to pick up some supplies. "Lily, I'm here." She carried the empty crate she'd brought for the bud vases she was going to use for her salon. When she moved beyond the pretty hostess stand, she stopped. It wasn't only Lily, but her friends Miranda and Cass also waited for her. A table was set with French presses full of steaming coffee, a bowl of fresh fruit and a platter overflowing with a selection of pastries. The intoxicating scent had her drooling and almost overloaded her instinct that something was up.

"Surprise!" Lily yelled.

"Uh...is this another ambush?" Her senses were tingling.

"I'm not sure Miranda's lemon Danishes say, 'Ambush' exactly." Lily pulled apart a pastry and took an enormous bite.

"Mm, well, what do they say?" Gabby raised her eyebrow and got into a stare-down with her best friend.

Lily caved. "We're a tiny bit dying to know what's going on with you and Luca?"

Gabby's mouth opened in shock. Why hadn't she come running into their arms right after her relationship had ended? Why had she even dated such a loser in the first place? Why had she been horrible at communicating all that time in L.A. and since she'd been home? Those were the questions she expected during this interrogation. And she had been expecting one. Her friends were too concerned and interfering to let her simply sneak back to town with her tail between her legs and hide for too long.

"Come on. I was there yesterday when Luca appeared. I was nearly incinerated by the steamy look he laser beamed your way." Lily stuffed the rest of her pastry in her mouth.

"I...uh..." Gabby sat and poured herself some coffee. "You always make the best coffee, Miranda."

"I do, don't I?" Miranda gave Gabby a side hug. "But that was a weak attempt at changing the subject." Miranda poured herself some and swooned over the liquid gold. "Ahh, may my coffee be stronger than my baby's desire to stay awake all night."

"Cheers to that," Cass said. Like Luca, Cass and Adam Brockman had twins, only six months old.

"Although my pastries are good enough to torture someone into talking." Miranda gave a pointed look at Gabby over her mug. "We just miss you."

Gabby relaxed and lowered her guard. She'd never had it up around these women before California. "I'm sorry. I know I've been a horrible friend." She hadn't allowed herself anytime to sit with her heartbreak once she'd come home. She'd jumped head-first into working overtime for her mom's nail salon in Florence, saving money and finally signing the lease on her own space. Once she'd done that, she'd felt as if she could almost breathe again. On her own, little by little. She'd seen her friends since she'd come home, but she'd made sure to engage mostly in casual functions with lots of people so she wouldn't have to explain everything.

"You haven't," Cass said. "You moved to have a grand adventure. We loved hearing about it from afar. We cheered you on. But when things got bad and you disappeared off the face of the earth for a few months, we worried, even though you kept telling us you were fine. When you returned looking like someone had tried to crush the life and spark out of you, you made it obvious you needed time, and we gave it to you. But we're over that now. We're selfish. We want you in our lives, getting to know our families."

Oh, Gabby wanted that too, but it hurt. How could she tell them that? How could she tell them she'd never be able to have babies? And that the pain that came with that truth made it difficult for her to be in their happy spaces sometimes.

"Yep," Lily said. "No more time to brood and worry. You need our hugs and sass and friendship. We're going to smother you with it, make sure you know how much you mean to us." She licked the powdered sugar off her fingers, making loud smacking noises with each finger. "All we need in return is dirt."

"Dirt?" Gabby said, chuckling, relieved at the change of subject. She dabbed the tears away with her napkin. Only great friends could have her laughing and crying in the same second. It hadn't been about space, but about not wanting to talk about her embarrassment, her failures, her...lack of...everything.

"Yes." Lily fanned her face. "The sexy-laser-beam-eye-gazing transmitting the message, 'My body wants yours.' Luca Rossi dirt. I mean that man has it bad for you. I thought it was the heat, but it was waves of lust wafting between you two."

"You could tell all that from a few minutes?" Gabby smirked, but the flush rose on her cheeks. Lily wasn't far off the mark.

"Oh, honey, that man was wishing I was nowhere in sight. Wishing he had you alone in a locked room with an enormous bed where he could do a whole lot more than undress you with his eyes."

"He does have phenomenal eyes," she said and nabbed a pastry from the tray. Gabby had missed this wonderful group of friends, talking about life and love and sexy hunks. It was time to let them back in, to make an effort to be in theirs. She'd save her worst heartbreak for later. Maybe so much later as in *never*.

"It always starts with their eyes." Miranda sighed.

"And hands." Gabby grinned.

"There is so much to be said for a man who works with his hands, isn't there," Cass added.

"And lips." Gabby threw out the last bit while savoring a delicious bite of cinnamon sugar wrapped in layers of dough.

"Yes!" Lily squealed. "I knew it! And you barely just met. That man has good taste. Tell us about the kisses, every single one."

"Well...uh, there's only been one. Yesterday morning after you left." Gabby grinned and hid her face behind her mug of coffee.

"Right," Lily teased. "I can see how talk of the layout for Blossom Festival can lead to making out."

"Well...um, there wasn't much talking going on," Gabby said. They laughed with her. Goodness, it was fun to act giddy and chat about happy things. She hadn't felt she'd deserved joy for a while.

"Wow," Cass said, "I knew you had mad baking skills, Miranda, but did you inject these with a truth serum?" Cass inspected her croissant.

"I think the truth serum is you all. I hope you know my absence was never about any of you, but about figuring out how to trust myself. I made so many stupid decisions and it's taken me a while to lick my wounds," Gabby admitted.

"We get it." Cass took her hand. "But you don't have to do this alone."

"And whatever happens with Luca, honey," Miranda said, "he's a good man. He and Cruz have been friends for a long time. I'm not saying anything has to come of sexy flirting and great kisses, but he's no Johnny Jackass."

Gabby *so* should have come home earlier, come home to her friends, her family, her support group. "He's...I... To be honest, I'm still scared of getting involved, especially this soon. I gave up my salon dream, gave up myself for a man and it nearly destroyed me."

"It may have, but you dusted yourself off and you're starting over. That takes strength and bravery. We've all learned that in life." Cass grimaced.

"And we are here for you. In fact," Lily said, "after we eat, we three are coming to your salon to help you with any finishing touches before the opening. That's the real surprise."

Gabby was speechless. "I love you, ladies," she whispered and wiped the last few tears off her cheeks.

"Love you too, Gabby," Lily said. "Now tell us how good of a kisser Luca is while we eat. Next, think about what you need help with, because you have us for three hours of slave labor."

"That's right. The men have the babies today. I might have to pump at some point, but I'm all yours. I heard talk of a mural that needs finished painting?" Cass said.

"I can help you set up your books," Miranda added. "I have a great new software that makes the accounting a breeze. I don't do too many clients these days, but you're special."

"I'd love that," Gabby said.

"You can put me to work wherever you need me," Lily added. "And can I ride over with you? Turner has my truck this morning. He's picking me up later downtown so I can take him to the airport. Gah! Berlin for two weeks. I'm going to miss him."

"So no sexy kisses for you for a long time?" Gabby teased her friend.

"I know." Lily pouted and took another Danish. "It's horrible. I might not survive." She yawned. "Maybe I'll take a two-week long nap until he returns. I could really use a nap."

"Come on," Gabby said, tugging her friend out of her seat as Cass and Miranda took the dishes to the kitchen. "Are you sure you're feeling okay? I've never seen you nap in my life?"

Lily hurried out of the door ahead of her. "Fine, I'm fine. Maybe too much work, as you said."

Huh? Weird. Not only has work never been a problem for that go-getter, but even if it was, she'd never complained about it. Gabby shrugged off the thoughts and joined Lily outside.

"Well, if you're up for it, I need your help on converting an antique cupboard to a nail polish display case. Then you can nap all you want."

Chapter Fourteen

"Lily, wake up." Gabby nudged her friend's shoulder. Lily had fallen asleep on Gabby's soft new sofa that she'd brought in for the waiting area of the salon. It was one of the funnier things Gabby had seen. One second Lily had been sitting up and texting, the next she'd fallen over sideways completely asleep. "Turner's on his way, he texted you."

True to their promise, her friends had stayed and helped for hours. Cass had finished the leaf mural on one wall near the front door. Enormous teal green leaves made the area pop. It was a sensational accent wall, if she did say so herself, and even better with the curved 1920s orange sofa in front of it. She'd traded out the simple white pendant lights for these big round gold sparkly ones that looked like dried shimmering dandelion poofs. And they'd hung a few planters on the walls to fill with green plants.

The few splashes of color felt amazing. What in the hell had she been thinking with an all-white palette?

The bright additions made so much more sense today with Cass, Miranda and Lily here, filling the space with their chatter and laughs, their oos and ahhs over how excited they were to see it when it opened.

The mural had taken shape while she'd had a quick training on the accounting software. Miranda had put small green glass bud vases at each hair station and Lily had worked her magic on the nail polish cabinet, now painted silver and showcasing all the polish colors as if they were jewels. It was each addition to the space, but more than that, it was her people bringing joy and delight back to her life, bringing her back to her center, her truth.

Lily dragged her head up and wiped her eyes. "For crying out loud, I've never been this tired in my life. What are you doing to me?"

Gabby laughed. "Are you talking to me or talking in your sleep?"

"I'm talking to the alien."

Gabby studied her friend and felt her cheek, warm but not feverish. "Alien? Are you sure you're not sick?"

Lily grimaced. "Ugh, nope," she mumbled and chugged from her water bottle. "Not sick. Uh, can you keep a secret?" She was whispering even though it was only the two of them in the salon. Cass and Miranda had both rushed out with boobs full of milk for their babies. Both women were complaining but also excited to get to their kids when they left. And Gabby had wondered if she would have been that kind of mom, annoyed that her shirt was wet from breast milk, and in love with her babies anyway. The pain squeezed her heart, and she stuffed it down deep where it belonged.

"Sure, Lil, what's going on?"

Lily faced her, eyes wide, mouth pursed before she said, "I'm pregnant."

The words fell like stones in her gut. Gabby's heart collapsed and rolled inward, hiding its tears from the world once again. She wasn't sure what the expression on her face said, but it must not have been great because Lily rushed on.

"Only barely seven weeks. I found out yesterday afternoon...I...I wanted to...we, Turner and I, wanted to keep it between us for a little bit. It's so special, but world-altering. I feel like someone's dangling me upside down over a cliff and I'm swaying in the wind. I didn't even know if I wanted kids." She squeezed Gabby's hand so tight it hurt. "I mean you know that. We were always going to be single and childless forever. I'm so scared." Her last words were a choked whisper. Tears leaked out from Lily's eyes.

"Oh, my friend." Gabby forced the words out along with a smile. "I'm so happy for you." And she was, even while her own insides felt raw. The truth was she was both messy emotions at the same time. Her own tears fell as she wrapped Lily in a hug. "This is amazing. You're going to be a mommy."

"Can you even fucking believe it? Me?" Lily laughed through her tears.

"Honey, are you not aware of how wonderful you are at taking care of the people around you?"

"I guess I do okay, huh." Lily sniffed.

"You must really have an alien in there if it's messing with your confidence."

"It's so huge, you know."

"Yeah," she lied. What did she know? Absolutely nothing. And she never would.

"I'm glad I told you."

"Me too." She forced meaning into the words. She did mean it. It was just clouded over by her own sadness.

"Oh, Turner's here. I have to go." Lily jumped up and grabbed her bag and her tool kit. "I need him to stop and get me a lemonade smoothie. This alien craves lemon like you wouldn't believe. Love you, talk soon," she said and raced out of the door to Turner's arms.

"Love you too," Gabby whispered to the empty salon. She didn't let herself rest or collapse. She couldn't. She found the broom and began sweeping the dust and debris she and her girls had created. The chore was what she needed right now to push forward through the pain. Cass had said Gabby didn't have to weather her traumas and tragedies alone. Really that was only partly true. There were some areas Gabby would always be completely devastatingly alone in. Even in the best circle of friends.

* * * *

"Hey there." From outside Luca had seen her sweep her salon with a vengeance attacking the dust like a wronged warrior out for blood. She hadn't lightened up when she moved to the mop. He was worried about her floors. She whipped around toward him, her face covered in ruin before she wiped the emotion away, mostly. Traces still lingered in the lines of her forehead and in the sorrows under her eyes. She mangled a smile, and he could literally feel the anguish shrouding her like the humidity on a summer day in the deep south.

Drowning was the word that immediately came to mind. *She's sinking and she needs help.* He set the plant he'd brought her on the reception desk and was next to her in a heartbeat. "Hey, everything okay?"

"I...uh..." She shook her head. "I..."

Luca took the mop from her hand and walked it to the storeroom. He rinsed it out in the work sink and tilted it up to dry. When he returned Gabby was rubbing her eyes. She crossed her arms over her chest.

"Sorry...I'm... Long day." She glanced around the room as if she was realizing where she was. "What time is it? What are you doing here?" She looked less out of it when her eyes found their way to his, but her voice had a hollow note to it.

"Four-thirty. I was on my way to pick up the girls, but I had something for you. Forgot to give it to you...um...yesterday morning. Got distracted kissing you." Luca brushed his fingers across her cheek.

"Distracted, huh?" He breathed a bit easier when she nudged his hand with her cheek, and let her arms fall to her sides. "Our kiss seems forever ago," she whispered.

"Mm-hm," he said. "And yet, clear as a bell to me." How easy it would be to get lost in her again, to pull her close and resume that sunrise explosion that still buzzed through him. But he suspected that wasn't what she really needed at this moment.

"Here, I was pulling plants for a few of my jobs when the delivery trucks were at the nursery. I... This reminded me of you. It's your favorite color, I think."

That got a smile out of her. "It's so pretty, Luca, and thoughtful. Thank you." She fingered the leaves. "What is it?"

"Maidenhair Fern. Silly name, but there something about it that caught my eye. It's delicate, but strong, dynamic. I've gone to bed every night this week thinking about you. Wake up with you on my mind too. Didn't get a chance to tell you that yet either."

"Luca," she whispered.

"Too much?"

"I… It…" She hesitated then shook her head.

God, I wish I knew what was wrong. Risking rejection, he twined their fingers together. She looked down and studied their connection. She reminded him of an animal who'd been beaten down one too many times, shy to trust, wary. But when he drew her body into his for a hug, she settled into him as though she belonged there.

He breathed out his relief. Something about Gabriella had his instincts kicked into high gear, urging him to be open and direct, all the while knowing she might run. His chest expanded, really expanded for the first time in years. Ever since Noelle died, he'd been a cautious man, soldiering on and planning for stumbles around every corner. Keeping his personal life contained because getting close to people meant they could leave you.

But with Gabriella, he felt so many things—joy, attraction, hope, protectiveness, anticipation. She eased a burden, hell, an entire fortress of stress inside him. Not to mention heated his blood with desire. He'd already mauled her once this week in broad daylight. It had riddled his brain long after he'd driven away. Afterward, he hadn't had the most productive day, but he couldn't say he minded the reason why one bit.

"I have to get the girls. Are you sure you're okay?" He didn't want to let go.

She tipped her chin. "Mm." She closed her eyes and shivered, and he could swear she was somewhere else. "Nasty demons coming back to haunt me."

"Anything you want to talk about?"

That pain flashed over her eyes, dampening the gold before she shook her head. Disappointment flinched in him. He was being irrational. They barely knew each other.

"Wow, that corner." Luca took in the wall with the enormous leaves and soft orange sofa with the scalloped back and slight curve to it.

"Yeah, what do you think?"

"It's amazing. Did you do it?"

"I drew the flowers. Cass painted it for me today. I found the sofa years ago and had it in storage. I'd completely forgotten about it." She walked to the wall and gently brushed her fingers over it. "It's a statement all right."

"A damn good one."

Talk about damn good. She was so pretty when she blushed, especially when it reached her eyes and they glazed over.

"Luca, you make me feel lovely. The things you say."

"You deserve to feel lovely. You should be proud of that, of your ideas. I know I'm impressed. Plus..." He leaned in and kissed her cheek, let his lips linger, felt her breath hitch and his own intake when she gripped his waist. "Plus every time I compliment you, your cheeks get rosy. It lets me know exactly how you're feeling."

She gripped his shirt around his waist and rested her head against his chest. Every silent thing about her said she was exhausted. He wanted to kiss her, but he also wanted to be the support she needed for whatever battle she fought. The thought didn't scare him the way it might have a year or two ago. Time might have made him stronger since Noelle's death, but it felt like more than that. It felt specific to this woman in his arms. He wanted to cherish her, prove to her that he was someone she could lean on.

"Come over and have dinner with us? Nothing fancy." He rubbed her back, settled into the warmth of the moment. "Might be chaotic. I want to offer you a glamorous date first. It feels like we're doing things out of order, but my life's kinda crooked and I can't say I mind the out of order. What do you say? A casual night. Let me feed you. Let my girls make you smile? Come enjoy my family."

When her eyes met his, with her face unguarded, both softness and turmoil exposed for him to see. "I don't know, Luca...I...should stay. I have so much left to do."

"You have to eat. Can't open a salon on empty."

"True," she said.

He could see her processing things, then finally a smile.

"Okay."

Something inside him swelled and burst. It scared the shit out of him. But some of the scariest life moments were the most amazing. And he was certain this woman in his arms was as precious as they come. Already he could see her in his life, in his daughters' lives. This was so much more than a simple fling for him.

Chapter Fifteen

Gabby heard running feet and screams before the door opened. And when it did, she had to fight back the tears from a heavy emotional day at the sight that met her. Luca, freshly showered with his hair still lightly wet and messy, in bare feet, wearing shorts and a navy short-sleeved T-shirt showcasing his powerful arms, especially since he was straining to hold one daughter under each arm like he'd scooped them up around their waists to run wild with them.

Emi and Tess were laughing and trying to scream, "Gabby!" at the same time.

She might crumple right there. She should turn right around and run from all this beauty. She wanted to walk right into it. Hovering on the doorstep, on the edge of so much *more*, it was a good thing they started talking and cut through her fears, at least for now.

"They're not supposed to answer the door without me," he said, giving each girl his stern raised eyebrows, even as the smile warmed his face.

"But it's *Gabby*," Emi squealed. "We knew who it was because you told us, Daddy."

"We're supposed to practice being safe, anyway," he said and set them down. They rushed to her and instinctively she crouched and held out her arms. Before she knew it, she was enveloped in little girls, both of whom were speaking to her at the same time.

"Gabby, you came! To our house. Want to see?" Emi said. The little girl could barely contain her excitement, bouncing on her toes, eyes wide and smiling.

"Here," Tess whispered and handed her a plush stuffed unicorn. "In case you get nervous, and you need a safe pal while you're in someplace strange."

"Girls, let her up, sillies. Then we can show her around and feed her. Remember I told you she had a tired day?"

Emi and Tess stepped back a mere fraction of an inch, studying Gabby with forceful eyes as if she might disappear in a puff of smoke at any second. Luca held out his hand. She was capable of getting up herself, but she put her hands in his regardless. He was always there, helping her, and right now while her heart was once again smashed into a million beautiful and difficult pieces, she was grateful for the help, but more, the warmth and connection that zinged through her with his touch. It soothed some of her broken parts. His smile soothed her too, right out of her funk. He was so beautiful.

"Nice apron." She kept a hold on his hand and roamed her eyes over his chest. The pink apron fit him well. It had flowers on the pockets and right over his chest were embroidered the names *Emilia Grace* and *Tessa Rose*.

"We made it!" Emi jumped up and down, ran into the house and returned with two small aprons in her hands. "Nonny helped us before she went on her cruise. For his birthday so he wouldn't get spaghetti sauce on his clothes. She pulled her own pink one on over her head and handed Tessa her blue one. "We made ones for us too. Oh no," she cried. "We don't have one for Gabby."

"We have plenty of extra aprons, Emi, but tonight Gabby is our special guest. She is going to relax, and we are going to cook for her."

"Can we show her our house first, so she knows where everything is?" Tess asked.

"If she wants a tour, then you girls can give her one." Luca quirked his eyes at Gabby, humor simmering inside them.

"That sounds lovely," she said.

"Pretty bracelets," Emi said, fingering the series of mismatched gold bands Gabby had placed on her wrist.

Gabby had raced home to shower and change into shorts and a cute summer blouse. She was exhausted but the thought of eating dinner with Luca and his girls wrapped around her in comfort. *"Casual,"* Luca had said. And she was, but that could also mean pretty, especially if one was maybe trying to impress someone. And she wasn't ashamed to admit at all that she was. Just, at this moment, she wasn't quite sure if it was Luca or his daughters.

"You can go barefoot if you want," Tess said.

So Gabby kicked off her flip-flops, set her purse down, handed Luca the bottle of wine she'd brought and held her hands out for the girls. They led her upstairs and when she sent Luca a smile over her shoulder, he was still there, watching her with such intensity on his face that hit her full-on in the sternum, nearly knocking her off her feet with the heat of it.

Gabby managed not to trip and faceplant into the stairs. Somehow, she took a deep breath and disappeared with two little curly-haired fairies.

* * * *

"So how was the tour?" Luca handed her a glass of wine when she stepped out onto the deck with the girls. They ran off into the yard with their arms full of stuffed animals and a blanket.

"Well, I did get to see where the bathrooms were, thanks to Tess. In case I had to go really bad." Gabby chuckled and Luca's face warmed and softened. "Then I got led right into the very important sanctuary of their room. I suspect that's what the tour was about."

"Yeah." He took her hand, pulled her to him and set a quick light kiss on her lips.

"Luca, you've done such a good job with them." Gabby placed her hand over his heart where their names rested.

Something profound flashed in his expression, but he turned back to the grill, keeping her hand in his and tucking their hands between them so they were aligned side by side.

"Hey, you don't think you've done a good job?" She craned her head to see his eyes and saw the flush in his cheeks.

"It's hard to know, doing it alone." He cleared his throat and focused on flipping the chicken. When he met her gaze, his eyes were clear and dark, intent and maybe a bit overwhelmed. "I always wanted to be a dad, but it feels like a fool's errand most days. There's a hint of instinct, but mostly it's what the heck am I doing?"

"Mm." Gabby leaned into him, resting her head on his shoulder as they both stared down the chicken breasts on the grill. Luca used the tongs to remove them and set them on a platter. He shut off the gas and she let herself be brave and say what she thought.

"I'd say it's way more than a hint of instinct, based on what I see. Also, I think your instincts are amazing." She'd never thought much about how difficult it must be as a single parent.

He captured her lips again, then let go of her hand to wrap his arm around her and hold her next to his side. This kiss wasn't quick or soft. It was heavy and full of meaning. He dove his tongue in and plundered her mouth. Gabby sucked in her breath, leaned up on her tiptoes and held on.

"Thank you." He held her there, on her toes, tight against him as he spoke.

"For kissing you?" she teased quietly.

"For your words. Makes me feel good to hear what you think. Goes deep." He placed his hand over his heart.

"Luca." She gripped his biceps. "You hardly know me. Why does what I think matter so much?" Confusion swirled inside her, confusion and a hint of fear or excitement? Why was it difficult for her to tell anymore? She wanted to be certain. They'd shot from casual to intense in a heartbeat.

"You matter." His words were an oath, demanding that she believe him. "And I know some things." Wow, he was so serious, almost angry. "I know you're full of dazzling light. I know you've been lovely and more than kind to my girls since the first time you saw them, even when I was a jerk. You didn't take long to forgive my gruffness and let me be a different man. You treat them like every word, every action, every emotion inside them matters. You've welcomed us into your beautiful family, trusted us to embrace them.

"When I spilled my guts, you listened and took care with my wounds. You're vulnerable with me. That's a layer of trust you've already given me, Gabriella. You can't take it back. None of it. And all of that has nothing to do with your amber eyes that speak their own language to me, and those sexy as hell legs I can't wait to have wrapped around me. When you're ready."

Their hearts thudded together. It was the only sound she could hear tunneling in her head. Gabby couldn't breathe, could barely speak. She shook her head, letting some air reach her lungs. "I thought you said this was casual," she whispered.

"Our clothes, maybe," he teased, and his face grew tender with his smile, but those eyes of his still swirled with intensity. "Truth? Nothing about you and me feels casual, or at least not only casual. Can people be serious and casual at the same time? Be everything?"

She would never be everything for someone. Gabby put her hand over his mouth. "You have to stop being incredible, Luca. Cool it. I can't handle it." She tried to play it off by teasing, but she really wanted him to stop. What would he say if he really knew…knew there were parts of her she could never heal? That she was flawed, less than other women.

"I disagree. I think the Gabriella you've shown me glimpses of can handle anything. And she deserves to handle the amazing. Besides, I'm simply speaking the truth as I see it, feel it."

Gabby's eyes flicked between his, listening to his words, but also the silent language he gave her with that deep strength of his. She so desperately wanted to believe him. What harm could it do to believe, even just for a little bit? Slowly she slid her shaking hands around his neck and linked her fingers together. "It's a good thing you're holding me up," she whispered.

"I feel the same," he said before he gave her one last gentle kiss, fitted her to his front and faced the yard with his arms wrapped around her. "The two most precious things in the world to me are right there." His low voice brushed against her ear.

Emi and Tess had set their animals up and were trying to use sticks to make a tent out of their blanket.

"Found another precious gem here in you, Gabriella. I'm not letting go. Not unless you tell me to."

Gabby held on to his arm with one of hers, and with the other she wiped her tears, the emotions of the day overwhelming her. She should. She should tell him to let her go now, before they both got hurt, but it felt so lovely in his arms with his words weaving their way into her heart. "You're not going to cool it, are you?"

"I don't plan on it, no. Before Noelle, before the girls, if I wanted to accomplish something, I set my mind to it, and I did it. Last few years I've been living in a blur, letting things happen around me. Tired of that shell of a man. It's time to go for what I want again."

He won't mean that when he finds out the truth. She was so tired of the confusion in her head, in her heart.

"I think we could both use some amazing. Feels like I'm holding amazing in my arms."

"Yeah?" she whispered. It was difficult to get the word out. He certainly was. Believing it about herself was infinitely harder to do.

"You know what else this is?"

"I might be afraid to ask," she admitted.

"A great first date, even though we're standing barefoot in my overgrown yard with two girls about to lose it because their tent keeps falling down."

Gabby laughed. She untangled herself from his arms and from her unsettled emotions. "I agree." She gave him a soft kiss. It was the truth. They were having a lovely time and she wanted to hold on to that, simply that for now. Then she jumped off the porch to go help his daughters.

* * * *

The lazy half-moon was already visible in the inky sky as Luca walked her out to her car. "Shame I have to say goodbye to you so early, but I intended this to be an easy night for you, one where you got pampered. Building blanket tents and putting two girls to bed doesn't exactly say relaxing," he said, chuckling. He leaned against her car and spun her into him.

Exhaustion hovered under her skin, dragging at her, but she was also overflowing with joy. The evening had washed away her pain. "It was hardly putting them to bed." She laughed with him. "All I did was read them a book. I'm pretty sure they were both deep asleep before I finished the second page."

"Mm." He rubbed her arms. "You also tucked them in and kissed their foreheads, both huge actions."

"You were spying? Didn't think I could do it, huh?" she teased.

Maybe he didn't? *Oh, no.* Of course, she was just a random woman who'd never had kids. Luca had done everything, grilled chicken, fixed a delicious salad and some plain noodles with butter. After he'd finished, he'd brushed the girls' hair, while Gabby had observed and giggled. Somehow through their protests, he'd gotten their jammies on. Emi, no surprise, had spoken a mile a minute the entire time, most of which Gabby understood. And Tess had sneaked little smiles her way.

"Not spying. I had no doubt you'd be awesome at it. I just wanted a first-row seat at the special magic weaving between you and my girls."

He held her close and kissed her, and Gabby let go and melted into him. All this talk of magic was working its way under her skin, lingering around the bruises in her heart, pushing her.

She slipped her hands under his shirt and roamed them over the tight muscles of his back, along the ridges of his spine. *Such an amazing spine.* And that was a first, wanting to memorize someone's spine. He let out a moan, reached down, slid his hands into her back pockets and grabbed her butt. His lips were everywhere, skimming the delicate needy skin of her neck, teasing along her collarbone, melding with her lips. While her skin was on fire and her blood hummed with his name and the plea, *more, more.*

He moved one hand to her lower back and pressed her into him as if she wasn't already trying to be one with him. The other he snuck to the ripped hem of her jean shorts. He teased under the fabric with his thumbs, along her thighs, to the lower edge of her panties then right there on her inner thigh.

"Oh." The jolt of lust seared through her.

He did it again, almost, *almost* along her seam.

She could close her eyes and imagine, and the imagining was so good in itself, fantasizing about him going higher. Right there to where she needed him most. When his thumb stroked her, she whimpered into his mouth and snaked one leg around his thigh, opening for him.

"Wet for me already, Gabriella."

Why was it such a turn-on when he said her full name? She was drenched and aching for him.

"Bet I could make you come right here," he whispered low and dark.

Fuck. She urged her hips into his touch. The man could go from cute dad to sexy, growling hotness in seconds. "Please."

Luca spun them so her back was against her car, then he put all that concentrated focus on kissing her. Well, not *all.* Holding her head with one hand, urging his body into hers, teasing his tongue into her mouth, he pressed his thumb against her clit, urging her higher until she burst, right there in his arms under the stars and dark sky. "Fuck." He gripped her. "You are so fucking gorgeous."

Gabby clung to him as her body shuddered and slowed.

Finally, he took a deep breath, buried his head in her neck and held her tucked in tightly.

"Luca," she whispered. *I knew he had amazing fingers.* Then a giggle burst out of her. They were wrapped around each other, cradled in the night as the crickets played their haunting song.

"Okay?" He smoothed his hands over her back and studied her face. "Gonna let you go home before I have you naked here on the grass for me."

Whew, I think I came again. "Luca Rossi, you should come with a warning sign for the ladies." Gabby fanned her face and almost tripped when he opened her door, holding her hand while she climbed into her car.

"Only you. No other ladies," he said.

He whispered a soft goodnight and shut her door and it was all she could do to drive away carefully without stopping and begging him to let her stay forever. But that was something she could never do because she wasn't meant to be someone's forever.

She managed to only glance in her rearview mirror twice. Both times he was standing there watching her. Could she really do this? Date a man like Luca Rossi, a man who deserved it all, knowing she would never fit into his dream?

Gabby worried as she drove home, her emotions and body overwhelmed.

Chapter Sixteen

Luca had imagined loving his new job. Owning his own landscape company. Having a say, *the* say in what mattered, actually being able to create his own designs and implement them. He'd anticipated issues new companies had. Added to that was starting a new business in a new city with new people and new weather patterns. New everything for him and his girls. He'd imagined getting dirty, having to dig compost out from under his nails, trying to figure out new native plants and diseases. He'd planned for so many pros and cons of this new venture.

What he hadn't anticipated was how distracting it would be to be working on Main Street all day out in front of a gorgeous woman's salon who had snuck into his heart and had his libido on overdrive.

She'd beaten him to work this morning, which wasn't difficult considering he had two tired girls to get to school and a nursery to visit to load up plants before he could make it into town. But what a sight he was greeted with when he parked his truck across the street from her salon.

She was on a stepstool washing the front windows, another pair of sexy shorts on and an old T-shirt, torn at the neck, showing hints of her tattoo. She'd tied the shirt off to the side in a knot, carefree, lazy and sexy as hell, showing off the smooth skin of her belly every time she reached the mop over her head.

She hadn't noticed him, and he took a moment to fill his brain with images of her. Those long legs of his dreams, flip-flops on her feet. He was too far away to see, but her toes were most likely the same shade of teal as last night.

She paused her sweeping and met his gaze. Her face softened and she gave him a cute wave with her fingers. Then the most enormous yawn took over her face. She covered her mouth and when it was over, even though he couldn't hear it, he could see her laughing and shaking her head.

Another beautiful spring morning. Still quiet on this downtown street, the scent of flowers from the bed of his truck, and a million tasks to accomplish today. But there she was. He should get her a coffee.

Drawn to her, he crossed the street to her open doorway. "Morning," he said. "Late night?" He wanted to walk right into her, wrap his arms around her, feel her warmth against him and breathe in her sexy scent. But he wasn't sure of the protocol yet, what she wanted and didn't want, what she expected, who she wanted to know about them. Plus, he needed to get to work. And if she felt as soft and warm as she looked, he'd be sweeping her off her feet and carrying her off to a bed right this minute.

"Not that late," she said. "I couldn't sleep." She stepped down and set her mop against the window.

"Excited about your opening?"

She nodded. "Mm, that and..." She crossed to him, took his hand, studied their joined fingers as she rubbed her thumb over his skin. "I was thinking of you."

He tugged on their connection "Didn't mean to keep you up?" His other hand went to her side, and he fiddled with the tie, brushing his knuckles across her bare skin.

"Oh, didn't you?" She wiggled her eyebrows and smirked, and damn that was cute as hell on her. Did she have a clue what she was doing to him? She must, as with each pass of his knuckles, she wiggled closer to him.

"No." *Fuck it.* He dragged her toward the back of her salon into a small nook. He walked her up against the wall. "Meant to give you sweet dreams." Luca leaned in and brushed his nose along her neck. "You smell so good. What is it? What is it about you, Gabriella, that gets under my skin and sets everything on fire?"

"I don't..." She leaned in and kissed his neck, grabbed his T-shirt by his waist and tugged. As if they could get any closer. "I don't know, Luca. You...you ma—"

Luca covered her mouth with his, swallowed her words. It was his name on her lips the way she hushed it out, a plea that snapped his control into bits. He had to taste her, wanted to devour her. The kiss didn't start out soft. It was fire and passion and unbridled need from the beginning. Her mouth was hot and wet, and he was willing to drown in her. She snuck her hands under his shirt, scraping those pretty-colored nails along his skin.

"Off," she demanded then chased his mouth with hers again.

As if he'd move one inch farther from her than was necessary. He had to break contact to pull his shirt off and toss it on the floor, then he gave her what she wanted and kissed her. Fucking hell, her hands roamed over his skin and when she sighed, she did it with her entire body arching into him. But it wasn't enough — he needed to touch her skin, all of it, feel her chest against his. He gripped the sexy tie of her shirt, tried to undo it, swore, left the knot, and dragged it over her head in desperation.

Then he had to pause. She wore a simple purple bra, no lace or bows, but none of that mattered. "Christ, you're beautiful." It cupped her full breasts, pushed them together and lifted them in offering to him. He traced his finger over her chest, along the upper edge of her bra, felt her shiver. With a swipe he had one cup down, her breast bared for him. He stroked his thumb across her nipple. He dragged his teeth across the stiff peak and when she purred, he took it in his mouth and sucked hard.

"Luca." Gabby grabbed his head and held him to her.

He swirled his tongue, used his teeth to work her up. He watched her while he teased her skin, head thrown back, mouth open, pulse jumping under her skin, free and uninhibited. Tugging the other side down, he gave the other breast the same attention and she cried out. Her silky-smooth skin, her breasts aching for touch, her cries and purrs — Luca couldn't get enough. His blood thundered through him, and he returned to her lips in a messy needy kiss.

She snaked her hands under his shorts and underwear and gripped his butt. He was hard as stone and rocked into her, nearly coming when she moaned. The sound was so fucking sexy he sucked on her tongue and wished they were naked, no clothes between them, no barriers.

"Christ!" He lifted her. Closer, his body needed to get closer. That was his goal right this second. She wrapped her legs around him and he tried like hell to be careful, so he didn't hurt her against the door. He stroked his tongue along her lips, kissed her neck, sucked at her soft delicate skin there and used his free hand to tease her nipple between his fingers, tugging on it to elicit another moan from her.

Fuck. Luca tore his mouth from hers. He was going to lose it. He wrapped one hand around her neck, caressed her swollen lips. She opened her dazed and hooded eyes then captured his thumb with her teeth, bit down gently and sucked it into her mouth while she thrust her pelvis against him. That was what she wanted. So he'd give it to her.

Ripping his thumb from her mouth, he grabbed her wrists and locked them above her head. Then he kissed her, sucking and biting at her lips while he moved his hips into hers, her legs squeezing around him. Then her body stilled, head back, breasts thrust toward him, she froze for a split second before her entire body lost control and she came. Her core was all heat and beauty. It pulsed against his cock through their clothes as her orgasm exploded from her. And he couldn't wait to feel that heat when they were naked, and he was buried deep inside her.

"Luca." His name sounded sweet and dirty on her lips. "I can't believe…" She panted out her breaths. "I just came."

"That was fucking beautiful."

He dropped her hands and wrapped his body around hers. Gabby opened her eyes, her entire body sagging, pliant in his arms. Her smile was loopy and beautiful. "Wow," she whispered. Her heart thudded in time with his. He was still fucking hard. But this was all hers. Christ, he had to walk out of here at some point and get to work.

"Was that…um." She snuggled into him making his task of cooling off that much harder. "Was that what you meant by sweet dreams?"

Luca couldn't help the laugh that burst out of him. "Got lost in you. Hope that was okay. I came inside to ask if I could buy you a coffee."

Then it was her turn to laugh. "Well, sweet dreams and coffee. You sure have a way, Luca. That was…that was spectacular."

"It was," he agreed and lifted her chin so he could kiss her one more time, soft and slow and full of promise. "You gonna be okay to go out there and get back to work?"

"Are you?" She raised her eyebrow at him and rubbed her fingers along his neck.

Against every cell screaming in his body, he set her down and stepped away from her sweet tantalizing goodness. "You have a point."

"My thoughts disappear when you touch me," she whispered so quietly and seriously as if she wasn't certain how that made her feel.

"You say that like it's a bad thing?" He got in close, put his hands on her thighs. Maybe he wanted her to lose all thought. Then she couldn't be wary of what this was between them.

"No...not bad...I..." Her smile was soft, contemplative. Some heavy concerns riding that brain of hers.

"Gabby, you here?" Lily called from the front of the salon.

Luca tugged his shirt on. "Oh my goodness. What are we, teenagers?" The sensitive moment gone, Gabby giggled, shoved playfully against his chest and fixed her bra. He slipped her shirt over her head.

Shame. Mussed up and undone is a dynamite look on her. And that fucking giggle after she came.

"Be right out," she called. Then she placed a kiss on her hand and touched her hand to his cheek. Unexpectedly, because he sensed she was about to distance them again, she took his hand and pulled him along with her to face Lily.

He wasn't embarrassed in the least. And now he could cross off any worry he thought she might have been. Even better, he got to watch her gorgeous ass sway like she was bragging as she walked ahead of him toward her friend and his...uh...boss.

Luca cleared the dregs of lust out of his mind and put on his game face. *Not boss, partner.* He gave himself a reprimand. He really had lost all sense of place and time, centered only on her. What a powerful fucking place to be, lost in Gabriella Flores.

"Luca stopped by to see if I needed a coffee," Gabby said.

Lily glanced between the two of them. "How thoughtful of him," Lily said, a huge smile blooming on her face.

"I know, right?" Gabby removed her hand from his and fixed her hair. Her cheeks and neck still sported a deep blush. One that he could stare at all day. "Now shoo." She waved him away. "Tall latte with a hint of caramel, if you still have time?"

Did she just shoo me? She's even cute when she's bossy. He liked this loose and free Gabby. And right then and there he made the decision to put that expression on her face as often as he could. Win-win for both of them. Luca winked. "For you, I have all the time in the world. Lily, can I get you anything from Retro Coffee?"

Lily turned as he backed away toward the door. "I wouldn't say no to a big icy lemonade." She was still fanning her face and glancing between Luca and Gabby.

Luca was outside and one shop down when he heard them squealing, and that sound put a huge fucking smile on his face. Gorgeous day all right. His employees were hard at work, people milled on the streets, the bakery was hopping and a line stood out of the door at Retro Coffee. It turned out, he was absolutely ready to get to work, especially if that was how he got to start his day. He'd try not to worry about how important Gabby Flores already was to him, and whether or not she was on the same page.

Chapter Seventeen

"I think I want to go much shorter."

Miranda sat in Gabby's salon chair, hair shampooed and conditioned. Gabby ran her hands through Miranda's long black hair that went almost to her waist. Fun bossa nova music played at the perfect volume through the ceiling speakers and mixed with the sound of a client getting her hair washed by Gabby's employee Ivy and a few people chatting at the front reception desk. A few neighborhood ladies sat on the soft orange sofa.

"Really? Are we talking a bob, pixie short?" Gabby held Miranda's hair up, leaving a swath across her forehead to mimic bangs. Miranda would look fabulous with short hair. All the angles of her face would pop. It would highlight her eyes and full lips. Poor Cruz might not be able to pick his jaw up off the floor.

Her salon door was propped open, and the breeze sent a wave of fresh air flitting through the space. It twirled with the eucalyptus shampoo, the sharp scent of nail polish and the fresh hyacinths in the bud vases, not to mention the enormous bouquets of flowers people had sent to congratulate her. The bright pink jagged-edged and gorgeous peonies from her moms, the lilacs from the Brockman ladies and the stunning purple calla lilies from Luca. Well, she wasn't sure she could smell those from where she stood, but her heart fluttered every time she eyed them, towering high and proud on the table in the waiting area.

Gabby was on cloud nine. Actually, she floated above it. The salon had opened with only minor hitches. Maybe because she'd planned and planned and worked her ass off to get here, right here to this moment. Plus, she'd had so much help. She couldn't deny that, and she silently reprimanded herself for insisting she do it all on her own, because she was nothing without these wonderful people in her life who were willing to do anything for her. She'd definitely lost her way in Los Angeles when she'd pushed her support system away.

They'd started with a soft opening today with a few clients, booked in advance. But it was such a good idea Gabby felt, as the day had moved on, to make sure equipment worked in the moment, to use the new computer system, to learn how to handle walk-ins, and break times. If they were going to be this busy, she might need to hire more people quickly. Especially a receptionist to handle the front desk, because not only were people constantly walking in to say hi and make appointments, but the phone was ringing off the hook. Three hours into their first day and she was almost afraid to see how many appointments they'd booked into the future.

Thank goodness for family. Her dad, an introvert and possibly the quietest man on the planet who studied the effects of climate change on local animal species, had a secret talent of being able to field phone calls and remain calm. And he was having a blast taking appointments and bragging about the services at Salon Flores. Every once in a while, Gabby heard him laugh, and she swore he was charming everyone who called.

"It's so beautiful and perfect," Miranda said, reaching out and grabbing Gabby's hand. Her friend's touch centered Gabby. She took a deep breath.

"Not perfect yet. The nail area still needs something. I'm not sure what." Four pedicure chairs and water basins sat across from each other, farther back from the hair styling chairs. Beyond the pedicure stations were the manicure tables. Everything was installed and in working order, but it still needed something. Every time she thought up an idea, she quickly tossed it aside. She'd hung some simple art for today, but the frames were mere placeholders, nothing lasting, nothing that made the right statement.

Miranda fit her hand back under the salon cape and studied the area Gabby was talking about. "Well, it's fine from where I'm sitting, but I think I know what you mean. Needs a little moxie, if it's truly yours, doesn't it?"

"Yeah," Gabby said. The word moxie went straight to her gut. She was rediscovering her moxie and no one was going to smother it ever again.

"It'll come to you, something special."

And as soon as Miranda said the words, Gabby knew it was true. It didn't hurt to have that kind of belief from her friends. She'd met Miranda years ago when she'd first come to Graciella and fallen in love with Cruz Brockman. Uncertain of her own worth, Gabby had been there to support her. *Everything comes full circle.* A phrase she'd heard her entire life, but she felt the depth of it even more now.

"I think you're right, but thank you for believing in me," she said.

"Always," Miranda said.

"So," Gabby prodded, "are we going to rock Cruz's world or what?"

Miranda's smile was huge in the mirror. "I was thinking a fun bob, maybe with bangs to make my life easier right now—hadn't even imagined that extra goodness."

"Oh, honey, I think I've subconsciously been waiting years to cut your hair. Short, flirty, and love the bang idea. Maybe even a teal stripe down the side?"

Miranda let out a soft laugh. "Work your magic, my friend."

Maybe she did have some magic after all. Her friends certainly made her feel that way. So did what she'd achieved today, despite all the obstacles thrown her way. She'd done it, she'd opened her very own salon in her hometown, exactly as she'd been planning for years. It was all she'd ever wanted, and now it was hers.

* * * *

Beyond the tall glass windows, the setting was enchanting, straight out of a movie. Luca had to step aside and pause outside the salon. Everything was brilliant and shimmery. But Gabby would have stood out in the pitch-black of midnight. She was stunning. The salon lights had been turned low and soft candles scattered about gave it a celebrational feel. It was full of snazzily dressed people, holding drinks, talking and laughing. The door was closed, but it didn't fully keep in the noise. Jazz music came through the salon speakers, and he could hear snippets of conversation, glasses clinking and laughter. A room full of joy. All because of her.

Isa, Mary and Lily sat, heads together, on the sofa. Jake was there with a tall blonde woman who was currently scrolling her phone. He recognized Miguel and Roxanna, and a few others. Many were strangers to him. Tables were set with food platters, and they'd transformed the other front corner into a cozy bar. Cruz Brockman held Miranda's hand as they stood next to Gabby. On her other side stood Adam Brockman with his arm around his wife, Cassandra.

And Gabriella stood glowing in the middle of them all. Short creamy white dress, with a tie that went around her neck not only leaving her shoulders bare but making them look super sexy and showing off the curve of her flower tattoo before it dipped back behind the dress. The material was so simple. It floated into an A-shape to mid-thigh, then nothing between her long, shimmering legs and high-heeled bright peach sandals leaving most of her foot bare.

Luca took one last moment to fix his tie and breathe in the clean night air, to try to settle his nerves before he went inside. This night was monumental for her, and he was honored she'd invited him. Hell, she'd flipped his entire world upside down from the first moment he'd seen her. It still hadn't fully righted. And as she cast her smile on the people around her, he realized he was one hundred percent okay with that.

Cheers to new beginnings. Luca opened the door and joined the magic. She noticed him the minute he entered, her gaze zapping into his. A flicker passed over her face quickly, relief or surprise. Then her smile grew infinitesimally wider and changed to something charged with secret knowing, with desire. He wanted all her expressions, but the initial one tugged at his heart. Had she wondered if he wouldn't show? *Only someone who's been let down or worse walks with those reservations held tightly inside them.* That pissed him off for her.

"Luca, you made it," Mary said. Holding hands, Mary and Isa came to his side, and both gave him hugs.

"Gabby will be delighted." Isa fixed his tie.

"She sure will," Mary said. It felt like one mom was saying, *don't you dare hurt our girl,* and the other one was cheering, *go get her!* And he hadn't even met her father yet. It was senior prom all over again. Sweaty palms and nerves as he waited to meet his date's parents.

"She have a good day?" he asked.

"Mm." Isa nodded. "Fabulous. Even better now."

"Don't you look handsome." Lily sighed and patted her heart.

Luca chuckled and his nerves fled. "Thanks, boss."

"I'm not your boss, I'm your partner and don't call me that either, come to think of it. It'll sound really weird. Now go." She gave him a playful shove. "Go get your star."

"Hey." Gabriella's voice drew his attention. She was there by his side, offering him that intimate smile. And suddenly his nerves thundered back in. This was a woman who could mean everything to a man, this was a woman with power. She could snap his heart in two in an instant.

"Honey," Mary said to Isa. "Shall we go get another glass of champagne to celebrate our daughter's success?"

Then it was just the two of them. Luca took both her hands in his and leaned in and kissed her cheek. "You look incredible," he whispered and slowly dragged his lips across her skin. "Thank you for inviting me." There, those were words he could say in a crowd, in front of her family and friends. Rational conversation words. Not what his body wanted him to say. That he was desperate to know what she was wearing under that dress, that he couldn't wait to get her naked and find out, that he was going to need hours to ravish her skin, then never let her go.

"Silly man. Thank *you* for coming. You got a babysitter and you're all dressed up. And the flowers you sent, Luca — so beautiful." Her voice was a hushed whisper of awe. Her eyes glazed over as she studied him, and it took every ounce of strength he had not to mold her body with his and kiss the hell out of her.

"Trying to impress someone important to me," he whispered back, the two of them lost in their own little bubble. "Tell me how it went, your first day? I want to hear everything."

"It. Was. Phenomenal!" She punctuated each word with a squeeze of their hands. Everything about her, her skin, her eyes, her voice sparkled with the joy of it and the force of how pretty she was with that excitement and pride knocked him completely off his axis. "Want to…um…want to meet my sisters and my dad?"

"Yeah," he said. "I'd love to." He'd do anything for her, including face the gauntlet of loving relatives waiting to see if he was good enough for their star, as

Lily had said. He'd never in his life wanted to be good enough so badly.

"Nervous?" she teased and led him to the bar.

"Like I said." He twined their fingers together and held her close. "Someone important." He saw the smile and the shiver run through her, and he had to talk himself down from getting hard right there in front of everyone. *She's going to kill me before we get out of here and I get to taste her.*

"Hey, Dad. There's someone I want you to meet."

Luca braced and tossed his erotic thoughts out of his head. *Focus, you're meeting her father.* The man was taller than Luca and broader. Silver hair, brown skin and dark brown eyes that grinned even before the smile reached his mouth. "Luca Rossi, this is my dad, Mateo Flores."

"Mr. Flores, nice to meet you."

"Call me Matty, everyone does." He gave Luca's hand a firm shake, sipped his drink and gestured to the three younger women standing around him. Two were behind the bar pouring wine and beer and one by his side. "Besides, Mr. Flores is the man who got called to the principal's office when one of these gems was up to shenanigans."

"Daddy!" The woman standing next to Mateo smacked his arm. The others, including Gabby, rolled their eyes and laughed. "We were perfect angels. Hi, I'm Amelia, the youngest and smartest." She gestured behind the bar. "This is Fran and Cammy. You already know Gabriella, I see." She gave him an inquiring look.

"And this is my wife, Julia." Mateo linked his hand with his wife's, who'd just approached them. "The real angel who saved me from going insane while raising a gaggle of daughters."

Julia chuckled and said, "So nice to meet you, Luca. It takes a brave man to walk into this family."

"Mom." Amelia sighed. "You'd think they had to come bail us out of jail every week."

Their easy banter and teasing made Luca feel at home. "I have two girls of my own, four-year-old twins, going on twenty-four."

"Aww." They gave out a collective sigh.

"They are adorable," Gabby said, leaning into his side.

As a family, they all watched Gabby with him and held their breath. And once more, he realized how necessary it was for him to treat her like gold.

"When do we get to meet them?" Cammy asked.

Just as Julia said, "Oh, do you have pictures?"

Luca took out his phone and they hovered around him, welcoming him into their fray. And Luca threw all caution to the wind about Gabby's stake in their relationship and stepped right in.

Chapter Eighteen

The entire night was starlight flickering across her skin. They'd only worked a short day, before everyone had gone home to change and the caterers had arrived. And Gabby rode on the cloud of high feelings the entire time.

Mary, Isa, her dad and Julia had come in when she was at home changing and they'd set candles all over the salon, some real, some electric. They'd brought in a small bar and hung lights over it. Their love added to the shimmer. Her friends and neighbors and cousins had shown, a few business owners in town and the entire Brockman crew, save Turner who was still in Germany.

Then Luca had walked in and a flurry of sparkles had bubbled up inside her like a new bottle of champagne. Everything else had fallen away, the chatter around her, the people, the drinks and amazing food. It had only been the two of them staring, while the wire between them sparked and cracked. It was a wonder she'd made it to him without tripping. Perhaps she'd simply floated to his side, buoyed by the emotions simmering between them.

He'd walked into the mess of her family acting as though he looked forward to it. And he'd met everyone in one night except for Javier, Isa's son, who'd left for a mission last month. She'd hardly gotten Luca to herself the entire evening. But aside from when he'd taken his phone out to show off Emi and Tess, he'd held her hand, fingers twined all night.

Now it was the two of them alone, under the real stars as she locked the doors. Nerves bounced inside her. Luca leaned against the window of her salon watching her. It was dark out, but it wasn't too late, a few minutes after nine.

"How...um..." She turned to face him, mimicking his stance, letting the window support her. She really was a jittery, floating bubble of champagne. Luca took her hand and inched into her space and she took a deep breath.

"How long do you have your sitter?" She wanted to spend the night with this man, take her time with him. She already knew a physical relationship between the two of them would be intense—she just had to keep reminding herself that was all it could ever be between them.

"Daisy's there till midnight. Can I take you to the new cocktail bar next to the pizza parlor? It looks dark and cozy." He brushed his hand across her cheek. "Intimate."

"I'd love that," she whispered, drawn to his touch, craving more. "But my car is at home and what I really want is for you to take me home, to come home with me. If you wa—"

He stepped in and kissed her before she could finish. *Nothing soft about it.* It was intent and heady, his mouth desperately mapping hers. He still held their hands between them, and he cupped the back of her head with his other, tethering her to him, kissing her deeply. She gripped his shoulder to hold on and felt his strong muscles. *So much control.* He ripped his mouth away, rested his forehead against hers, his breaths coming short and fast. Gabby moved her hands to his chest to feel the rapid thundering of his heart.

"I want." His words were desperate, a plea.

Maybe not so much in control. Her laughter flew off into the night as they sped-walked to his truck. He helped her up, gave her one more greedy, open-mouthed kiss, then shut the door and got busy driving. He took her hand in his.

"I feel like there are bubbles inside me. I'm ready to explode, Luca."

"Don't tease me, woman. I'm trying to drive safely here."

Thank goodness it was only a few minutes to her apartment. He walked behind her up the steps, holding her hips and whispering dirty thoughts in his low, sexy voice, and Gabby couldn't help the giggles. She didn't care who heard. She wanted the entire world to hear her.

She flicked on the small lamp right inside her door, and Luca dragged her to him, his mouth on hers before she was even steady on her heels. She kissed him with her own pent-up need, the live wire between them sparking higher with their connection as they tripped and stumbled to her bedroom. Gabby held on to him, trying to unbutton his shirt and shove it off along with his jacket. His hands were hot on her skin.

He brushed his fingers along her shoulder, toyed with the halter tie of her dress, sent tingles shooting through her whole body. "Been wondering all night," he said and placed a soft kiss on one shoulder, kissed her other, never straying far from the strap.

"Yes?" she whispered, tilting her head, giving him access, all the access.

"Wondering...been driving me crazy. Wanting to know what you had on underneath this."

"Mm." She shivered under his touch. "Not much." Her breath hitched as he played with the knot holding the dress up.

"This gorgeous back, teasing me. Smooth, silky, so pretty with the flowers inked into your skin." Luca walked her to her bed and slowly spun her around. She closed her eyes and felt his fingers tracing patterns on the bare skin of her back. From the tie at her neck, flicking his fingers under it, down over her shoulder blades, tracing her spine to where the dress dipped over her butt. A sliver of moonlight was all the light in the room, a mere strip across the bed. Everywhere else was hushed in shadows. He gripped her around the waist with one hand and smoothed his hand over her skin, so, so softly, and she ached for him.

"Luca," she whimpered, as he untied the halter and let it fall forward.

"Gabriella." Luca trailed his fingers around her neck, where the tie used to rest. The air hit her breasts, and she shivered under his inspection, the way he mapped her skin. Her nipples pebbled, so hard, aroused, waiting for his touch.

He kissed her neck, trailed his lips to her ear and whispered, "Can you feel what's between us? Is your body as needy as mine is right now?"

Placing his hands on her belly, he pulled her against him, his hard length pressing into her ass. She needed him, yes, she needed his bare hands on her skin.

"Yes." She nodded, rested her head against his shoulder and reached her arms around his head to hold on. *Finally.* He palmed both breasts, took her mouth and swallowed her whimper. He applied the same sweet, slow torture to her breasts, her nipples desperate for his touch. And when he teased his thumbs over the hard nubs, she tore her mouth from his and swore. "Again, please, Luca."

It was a good thing she was holding on because she lost all sense of balance when he gave her what she begged for. Using his powerful gorgeous fingers, he tugged on her nipples and a moan came from deep within her, surrounded by his heat, the scent of his skin as she breathed him in like he was the air moving inside her. Her body hummed as he stroked her higher. With each soft ache, there was so much pleasure. Her pussy responded as if it was connected to his touch, the way he played her, strummed her higher.

"I need to see you." Luca spun her again and gently pushed her onto the bed. "Fuck. Look at you. Dress around your waist, exposed to me. These legs." He lifted one and stroked his hands over it like she was a precious treasure he'd uncovered. He undid her heel and tossed it on the floor. "Silver sparkles."

"Wh...what?"

He set her leg down and took the other one, repeating his care. "Your pretty toenails. Swore I'd get near enough to see how you decorated them. Everything about you is a beautiful gift I get to unwrap."

Her breath came in short pants as he tore his shirt and jacket off. His eyes zeroed in on hers. He climbed over her, placed one hand above her on the bed and slowly teased his thumb around one breast, drawing circles closer and closer till he finally reached her nipple, taking all the time in the world. When it felt like she'd been waiting for him for forever. Then, while her entire body tingled under his caresses, he brought his mouth to one nipple and Gabby nearly shot off the bed.

Luca swore and palmed the other breast as she writhed and moaned under him. "You feel so good."

"*You* do, your touch. God, Luca." Gabby held his head to her as he sucked on one nipple, sending shards of pleasure through her as he bit and soothed with his tongue.

"Fucking hell!" Slow, controlled, teasing Luca was gone. He pushed himself up, knelt over her, and dragged her to him so her butt rested on his thighs and all he had to do was raise her dress and he would see how wet she was for him. Dragging his hands under the fabric, he worked it over her head, giving her chest a gentle push back down. She physically felt his eyes rake over her, searing through layers of shields.

"Tiny scrap of nothing." Luca set his searing gaze right on her pussy as he toyed with the fabric of her bikini, barely brushing against her body with the back of his fingers. Every brush was a promise of lightning. Then he lifted her, shoved the fabric aside and clamped his mouth down on her, sucking on her clit with desperation.

"Oh fuck!" It was her turn to swear. He drove his tongue inside her, sucked and kissed and devoured her. She shook as a ball of need rushed to her core, every nerve, every desire, every ache.

"Need to get these off."

"Oh," she pleaded as he tore his mouth away, moved her legs and dragged her panties off. "Don't stop." Thank the sex goddesses he wasted no time putting his mouth right back where she needed it. Sending long, desperate licks along her pussy, he watched her with hooded eyes. And his hands gripped her, marking her. Her body shook as she pumped her hips toward him.

He paused his tongue for a moment only to run his thumb over her swollen bud, coating her in her own juices, coating his thumb, slowly and teasingly, tormenting her with his intention. He did it again, carrying her along, urging her up.

"Luca!" with a cry she came apart, under his touch. He latched his mouth back on and sucked and tortured her, dragging her orgasm on into another one shuddering through her whole body.

"Beautiful," he whispered against her thigh, kissing her leg. Then he stood and undressed before her hazy eyes.

"You're the beautiful one. Come here." She held out her hand and he climbed on, nesting his body perfectly into hers. She kissed him, dragged her fingers through his lush hair, thick and dark, roamed her hands over his shoulders, down to his waist. She could feel the press of his hard cock between their bodies and she wanted more. "Luca," she said. "I've been dreaming of you inside me."

"Mm." He rocked his body over hers creating the most delicious friction. When he finally drew himself away to fumble through his wallet, he knelt on the bed, and she got to watch him. Cast in the barely there light from the living room and the moonlight as it streaked over his body. He rolled the condom on and stroked himself, big and beautiful and so hard. He braced his body over hers with one arm, while fitting his cock right to her entrance, still throbbing from her orgasm. She wrapped her legs around him and he nudged inside, inch by inch, filling her, stretching her.

"You feel amazing." With a mind of its own, her body arched toward his. "How hard you are...inside me."

"Fuck, I feel you clenching around me, Gabriella. So tight. So good."

He pulled out till the tip was the only part still inside her. Each tiny movement against her inner walls was a thrill, a spark. Then with one thrust, he seated himself deep again, repeating the motion over and over, driving his whole body, picking up the pace until he was drilling into her, his control undone.

"Fuck, so good," he growled, coming down over her. He wrapped his arms under her and cradled her head while he fucked her, keeping them melded together. Her hands fit perfectly on his wonderful ass and she tugged him to her with each of his thrusts.

"I need it harder, please," she begged, and he jacked into her, giving her what she wanted, their bodies grinding together in delicious friction. Everywhere his body touched hers sent her higher. She was shaking and when she came again in a hot explosion, she clung to him. For a second, he stilled, buried his head against hers and groaned out his orgasm, slapping into her thighs, until he collapsed on top of her.

"Christ, Gabriella." His breath panted fast and heavy against her cheek, his chest heaving into hers. She turned her head and kissed his full lips, soft and searching, so vulnerable suddenly. She clung to him while the magic slowed and loosened between them, and her body floated back to the bed.

"That was incredible. I mean…it…was more than that…" It was nothing like any time she'd had sex before. Never had the ripples of her orgasm lasted so long, completely depleted her. But also, she'd never had a partner's absolute intense focus on her, as if he sought every single way to connect with her. As if the only way for him to survive was to be one with her. She could barely catch her own breath. Words were meaningless. Or maybe it was the fear sneaking in and unthreading her self-confidence. Ignoring her worries, she held on and kissed him.

Luca rolled slightly to the side and cupped her cheek while they kissed, keeping them connected. "Yeah, a helluva lot more." He gently moved her to face him, resting his forehead against hers. "Be right back."

When he returned, he slid in next to her and tangled their naked bodies together, running his fingers through her hair. He studied every inch of her face, and a part of her wanted to hide from the scrutiny, but she didn't. She kept his gaze, let him see her. *Only the parts I'm willing to share.*

"Something special indeed," he said. He brushed the back of his knuckles down her chest, to her belly, over her hips, tickling along her side. When he stopped, he placed his hand over her heart. She did close her eyes then and fold into him, worried her darkness would turn him away. They stayed that way for minutes, wrapped around each other, holding on, coming down from the high. It was a pleasure to be held like she was precious and important.

"Thank you," she whispered.

He chuckled. "For mutual out-of-this-world orgasms? For letting me ravish this incredible body of yours?"

She laughed. "Well, there is that. But…" She studied his eyes, latched onto their strength. "No, for being so good to me, for listening, for taking care." Each word felt dragged from her, like someone who'd lost her trust, but wanted, wanted…what? What exactly did she want?

"This night was all you, Gabriella. You made it brilliant and I'm the lucky one who got to be in your orbit."

Gah! He keeps saying such lovely things. I want to stay right here in this second, where there's no past or future to worry over.

He tightened his arms as he spoke, rubbed his hands over her back, down to her hip and tugged it closer. "Wish I could stay the night, explore all my fantasies of you."

She softened at his words, allowed herself to enjoy, sent the worry fleeing from her mind. "You have fantasies of me?"

"Woman, you have no idea." He trailed his hand to her cheek, brushed her lips with his thumb and leaned in to kiss her. It was a slow kiss that moved from his entire body to hers, melted her.

"Wow," she said when he finally pulled away and stood, his naked body hers to take in. She had fantasies of her own and she hadn't had nearly enough time to explore his body, all his lean muscles and that butt. *Oh, baby.* "We're going to need a lot more nights like this one, then, aren't we?" The words were out, her brain loose and unfiltered before she could regret them.

Oh shit. Hesitation slammed back into her. Was he only interested in hot sex? Maybe that was what he'd meant the other night when he'd said they were both due some amazing. Or maybe he wanted so much more. Did it matter? *Yes, it matters.* Why hadn't she thought this through before tonight, before...*before letting my heart begin to bloom?*

Pants and shirt on, he sat on the bed and leaned over her. Smoothing her forehead with his thumb, he said, "Tell me what's going on up here?"

She pulled the comforter over herself and sat up. "I... Should we have...should we have defined what we both want, what this is, before diving in?"

Luca cupped her cheek again. Why did she love it when he did that? It was like he wanted her to know he was one hundred percent attuned to her every movement, expression, blink of an eye. As if she mattered.

"I definitely want more nights with you. I want stolen kisses in your salon, you over for dinner with my girls, date nights, sleepovers, families, holding hands and deep conversation." He grinned. "This isn't some fling for me. I don't think I can do that with you, Gabriella. You're too special for me not to want it all, to be all in with you. Even if our circumstances are a little tangled."

You have no idea. And suddenly she wanted to cry with that knowledge, her truth that would undoubtedly change things. She leaned into his touch and for the moment, tried to infuse her words with a sense of casual she no longer felt. "Tangled is my norm. Look at my wacky family tree." She tilted her head and placed her lips on his palm.

Luca dragged her to him and kissed her, hot and heavy and deep. He devoured her mouth, dancing their tongues together, stirring her up in a whirlwind of desire. She gripped onto his shirt to hold on. When he pulled his mouth away, his eyes were serious swirls of the ocean before a storm came. A warning of something with the power to be both astonishing and scary, if one cared enough to pay attention.

"Loved meeting your family. Can't wait to meet the rest. It's obvious they adore you. Look forward to learning more about them, about everything important to you."

"'Kay," she whispered, blown away by the force of him, his words, his kisses, his heat, the beating of his heart beneath her hand, the seriousness of it all. He was shattering her walls without even knowing what specifically they were. Reading her truths even if she tried to keep them hidden.

"Gotta get home to my girls. Don't want to leave you. So I'm gonna turn and walk away, before I lose myself completely and climb back in there with you."

"'Kay," she said again, her mind mush and apparently incapable of saying real words.

"Goodnight, Gabriella," he called before he shut the front door, leaving her completely freaked out.

Chapter Nineteen

Luca: Pretty sunrise this morning. Not as pretty as you.

Gabby was awake, lounging in bed with her coffee and her sketchbook, when Luca texted her. He included a photo of the sunrise over one side of his backyard. Captured in the shot but blurry were Tess and Emi racing through the yard with what looked like capes trailing off their bodies. Sweet, sweet man with two darling babies. *He's bound to want more.*

Gabby: Are those superheroes in your yard?

Luca: Yes. Princess superheroes helping save the garden fairies before the big bad lawn mower starts and scares them away with its roar.

Gabby: You have a challenging journey ahead of you.

Luca: Wait till I start whacking away and tearing out the blackberry vines. I might have anarchy on my hands.

The phone switched to him calling and she answered it with a nervous, "Hi." Ugh, why was she nervous? She'd had mind-altering sex with the man last night, sweaty and naked and so hot. Her muscles were still deliciously sore.

"Felt like hearing your voice. Not a great texter. Hope I didn't wake you."

"I've actually been awake for a while. Had a sexy dream of you and couldn't get back to sleep. Now I'm drawing." It was the truth. She might have gone to bed scared of what had happened between them last night, but her dream world hadn't been one bit worried. Too bad she couldn't just live in her dream world forever.

"Damn. You're killing me," he said, his voice low and charged.

And Gabby laughed, all her vulnerabilities whisked away with her breath.

"If I didn't have to go into battle with some badass superheroes, I'd let you describe this dream to me in great detail."

"Maybe we could rain check that."

"Yeah." Luca gave a soft sigh. "Had a great time last night, Gabriella."

"Me too," she whispered.

"Busy day?"

"Well, I made lots of notes about yesterday's opening. Need to figure out if I can afford to hire one more person sooner than I thought and get my sister on board for more hours. But I'm free in the afternoon."

"Want to come for dinner? You me and the girls again. It's still not the sexy date I promised you, but—"

"I'd love to," she answered quickly before her mind could freak out about what the hell they were doing. Sexy dates were certainly to be anticipated if last night was any indication of how Luca Rossi did them. From the minute he'd stepped into her salon party and twined their hands together, till the moment he left her apartment, he'd made Gabby the center of his attention. And his attention felt life-changing, which was exactly why she should have said no. "Can I help cook this time, or bring something?" Apparently, she was just charging head-first into a mess of her own making.

"Emi picked cheeseburgers. How does that sound? With my secret French fries which are actually frozen ones with a spicy salt that the girls love. And now that they're smart enough to know better, counts as a vegetable. Huh, I bet that's why Emi picked this for dinner. Schooled by the four-year-old. I've had to get more creative in how I get vegetables into them."

Gabby laughed. "Sounds awesome. How about I add a fruit salad to the mix? And maybe something fun for dessert. If you want them to have dessert."

"Yeah, perfect. After the girls go to bed, do I get to pick my own dessert?" His sexy tone had her squirming.

"Luca Rossi, behave yourself."

His chuckle sent more sexy shivers through her. "I need mental fuel to get me through my upcoming battle. Don't deny me, Gabriella."

She loved this, the soft laughter, the intimacy, the sexy talk between them, all of it. "Hmm. I guess I can't stop you from imagining," she teased. "I'm going to finish my coffee then step into the shower. See you soon, Luca." She sent a kiss through the phone.

"Not soon enough." His voice was a sexy threat.

After she hung up and tossed off her sheets, she didn't finish her coffee. But she did climb right into the shower with fantasies of Luca Rossi on her mind.

* * * *

It was four on the dot when she arrived. Gabby would have driven over right after their phone call this morning if that little voice in her head hadn't gotten the best of her. She was, after all, trying *not* to get lost in another man. She'd barely shut her car door when Luca was on her, pinning her against her car, tangling his hands in her hair and dragging her mouth to his. His kiss claimed her breath as he licked and sucked on her bottom lip, feeding on her, thrusting his tongue in to tangle with hers, obliterating any debate in her mind, any thought at all.

She stood on her tiptoes, whimpered as he pressed his entire body into hers, how tightly he held her head to his, the hard length beneath his shorts rubbing against her belly and zapping arousal right between her legs.

"Cruel woman," he growled and swallowed down her whimper with one more punishing kiss before he dragged himself away. His eyes were wild and hot and he was breathing heavily. So was she, after one short kiss. "Teasing me on the phone this morning." His gaze was on her lips as he brushed them with his thumb. She took it between her teeth, circled it with her tongue before he pulled it out and pushed it against her lips. "You. Are. Killing. Me."

"Where are the girls?" she asked, grinning at him. Anyone who looked at her would notice the dopey gaze on her face. Those bubbles tingled inside her.

Every time he touched her. *I wonder if he has them too? If when I'm near, the current sings through his blood.*

"Pretending to be buried under their stuffed animals so you'd have to discover them." He gave her a wry grin. "Come on. I'm surprised they lasted this long."

Luca took her bag in one hand and her other hand in his free one and led her into his home. Setting her stuff down inside his door, he put a finger to his lips and pointed upstairs.

She nodded and started up. "I wonder where Emi and Tess are?" she said loudly as she climbed. Giggles reached her before she made it to their bedroom door. Luca was right behind her, his hands gentle on her waist. *Oh my goodness, they are the silliest things ever.* Covering her mouth to stifle her own laughter, Gabby entered the room calling out their names. Each girl was hidden under a pile of stuffed animals. They were on the same bed, head to toe, each of their faces uncovered, and someone's toes poking out. Plus, every time they fidgeted or moved, the animals rose and fell, some shifted, causing gaps. "Look at these stuffed animals, what a comfy spot to sit. I think I'll—"

"Surprise," both girls squealed at the same time, wiggling their bodies and jumping out from under the pile.

Gabby gasped in mock surprise. "Oh, you fooled me."

The girls bounced on the bed and dragged Gabby into the soft pile of animals. She tackled them with her arms and tickled a few more squeals and giggles out of them.

"Your turn! Your turn!" Emi tugged Gabby down and Gabby dramatically let her.

"Daddy, we want her to stay," Tessa whispered.

"Yes! She could be our mommy," Emi said as she placed animals over Gabby. "Gabby, you could sleep in our room, and you could make more brothers and sisters for us. We want more kids!"

Her heart skipped a beat with her small gasp. From underneath the animals, Gabby sent a quick glance Luca's way. He was leaning against the doorframe, arms crossed, watching them with a soft grin on his face. When he caught her gaze, a look so powerful rolled through his eyes, a wave full of tenderness and love. She could feel it even without the spoken words. *Tell him, Gabriella. Tell him.* But in the next moment, the girls were giggling and falling on her.

"Save her, Daddy," Tess cheered, and Luca was there at her side to take her hand and lift her from the onslaught of toys and little girls.

"Who's hungry?" Luca asked. The girls squealed and scrambled onto his back. She let the worry slide away, let the warmth of his hand be her steady anchor for now. She needed to tell him, but she honestly didn't know how.

* * * *

Luca couldn't remember ever paying much attention to what women wore before. But Gabriella Flores sure did a number on him. This afternoon she'd paired a short-sleeved white blouse with deep orange shorts that tucked at the waist with a tie and curved out flirtatiously over her hips. Her entire body was wrapped in one big seduction package he wanted to explore and slowly tease her out of. Pull down one sleeve and kiss her shoulder. Run his hands over the slip of midriff he kept getting teasing glances of. And her legs—he couldn't take his eyes away from her long, silky legs. She was literally teasing him via clothing, and he was a drooling ogling dope.

"Look, Gabby. We got you an apron too," Tess said and offered the green apron with pink flamingoes on it to Gabby.

"It's not homemade, but it'll do for now."

"Put it on. Put it on," the girls chanted.

"Yes, let me help you." Luca lifted it over her head, carefully pulling her curls out from under the strap. He tried hard not to linger on the scent she'd dabbed behind her ears. He might have fiddled with the tie a bit longer than necessary, running his hands over the exposed skin where her shirt barely met her shorts along her lower back. "Looks good," he whispered and nipped at her ear as the girls scrambled to find their aprons.

Gabby gave a soft whimper and leaned into him.

Too fast for Luca, the girls were ready on their step stools at the counter. "Let's make dinner," Emi said. "I'll make the patties."

Luca sighed. "I'll make the patties, goofball."

"Can you help me make the fruit salad?" Gabby asked, jumping right in with them. She stood next to Emi and unloaded her grocery bag. Gold-hoop earrings shimmered next to her skin. He trailed his eyes down her neck over her apron-clad body, her curves now hidden. But he could imagine. He had a fantastic imagination. "We'll need a big bowl."

"It's in the pantry." Luca followed her in. She was inspecting his shelves when he nudged his body into hers, pushing her gently against the shelf. He ran his hands in between her apron and her clothes, reached under her shirt to her belly and held her tightly to him.

He kissed her neck down to her shoulder, loving how she always tilted her head to the side to invite more of his attention.

"Luca." She was as breathless as he felt. "I love it when you kiss my neck. How can it be so sensitive? What are you doing to me?"

As if she had to ask. She knew. *She knew* she was the one torturing him, fraying the last edges of his control. She had to feel it too, this unnatural fiery need between them now. She'd bloomed for him last night. There was no going back. Her hand clasped over his, too many layers of fabric between them.

"Daddy, are you kissing Gabby?" Emi squealed and ran out of the pantry giggling. Jesus, he'd lost complete control with his girls right on the other side of the wall.

Gabby's soft laughter hummed through her body, and he let the sensation wash over him before he stepped away. He righted her apron and brushed her hair into place.

"I'm helping her reach the sugar," he called. "Sorry," he whispered to Gabby.

"Really?" She smirked. "That look in your eyes doesn't say sorry at all."

"No." He kissed her quickly then started to walk away. "It says, I can't wait until the girls are in bed."

* * * *

Gabby tiptoed out of the girls' room and shut the door as quietly as she could, to be swept up in Luca's arms. Thankfully he kissed the surprised scream out of her mouth. "Shh," she reprimanded against his lips. "I finally got them to sleep."

"Hmm." He caressed her neck with his lips, and his smile warmed her skin. "Once they're out, they usually stay out."

He took her hand and they raced down the stairs and fumbled their way to his bedroom. He had his hands under her shirt and tossed it off her before he'd even shut his bedroom door. He kicked it closed and locked it. She was just as hungry for him as she dragged her hands into his shorts. He stole them away and wrapped them around her back, caging her into him.

"Uh-uh. I've been hard for you since you walked in here in this outfit—correction, since our phone call this morning. If you touch me now, it'll be over before I've had my fun."

"Your fun?"

"Yes, Christ, this body." He lifted her and she wrapped her legs around him as they fell onto the bed. He dragged her bra down and sucked in her nipple, and a current shot straight to her pussy.

"Luca." He sent thrills of pain and pleasure through her. When he ran his hands inside the back of her shorts and squeezed her butt, she attacked his lips, his neck, pulling at his shirt to get it off him. "I need to see you," she begged. He tugged his shirt off and tossed it, dragging her shorts and panties down her legs, kissing and licking his way between her thighs. He slowed then, as he kissed her inner thighs, smoothed his hands along her sensitive skin there.

"So ready for me." He dragged a finger over her pussy and teased her clit.

She arched and moaned under his touch, grabbed at the sheet and pushed her pelvis toward him, seeking his body. Every part of her ached for him. He crawled back over and ground his body into hers as they clawed and kissed and tried to burn each other down. She latched her legs around him again pulling him into her, mimicking the motion of their bodies fucking, even though the barrier of his shorts still separated them.

He tore at her bra till it was off in a tangled mess beside them. Holding her breasts like a wild needy man, he latched his powerful lips onto her other nipple, while she tried to get her hands in his shorts and shove them off. "Too many clothes," she whimpered.

"Don't move," he ordered, kicked off his shorts and ducked into the bathroom.

"Hurry," she begged, roaming her hands over her breasts, empty without him. When he returned, he already had the condom package ripped open and was rolling it over his hard cock.

"You're fucking gorgeous. Do that again, let me watch."

Her pulse kicked even higher as the pace of their actions slowed. She met his gaze and teased her hands along her skin, pinching her nipple and arching toward him.

"Lower," he growled as he stroked himself, towering above her, his eyes glazed with lust.

She gave him what he wanted, moving one hand between her legs, letting her knees fall open, she played with herself, rubbing her own wetness over her swollen lips, dipping a finger inside. It was too much, too powerful, and she closed her eyes, thrust against her finger, imagining it was him. In an instant it was. He climbed in beside her, tagged her around the waist and rolled her toward him, so they were side to side. And, lifting her hip over his, he thrust into her in one swift pulse.

She clamped her arms around him and held on while he rocked into her, his fingers teasing her clit. She bit her lip to keep from screaming when her climax smacked into her. Luca grabbed onto her hip, locking her to him. He picked up his pace and took her mouth in an all-consuming kiss as his own orgasm roared through him.

They clung to each other through the heavy breathing, the sweat on their bodies sticky between them. Both of their pulses hammered against their skin. Gabby could feel it all, relished it all, the frenzied need, the aftermath. Luca Rossi was a warrior at fucking her brains out.

"I think I'm dead," she whispered, and he chuckled, the vibration tickling her ear.

"Me too." He smoothed his hand tenderly over her hip where he gripped her. "Gonna get rid of the condom." He slipped out of her, then the bed and she rolled to her stomach. *Mm. I could watch him move for hours.*

He turned the bathroom light off, climbed over her and tucked himself in by her side. Leaning on his arm, he ran tender strokes of his hands over her body. He kissed her hip where his hands had dominated, trailed over the bumps of her spine, brushed her hair away from her shoulder and kissed the flowers on her skin. Everywhere his hands and lips touched her left a soft mark, better than any tattoo, the wave kissing onto shore then slowly rolling out. "That went fast." He brushed his lips across her chest.

"I'm not complaining," she said and smiled as the low laugh rumbled through him. Her head was turned sideways on the pillow, sinking into the sensations of his touch. She intended to spend time mapping his body the way he did hers. She dreamed of it, but right now in this moment, all she had the energy for was being pampered.

"Fast and amazing," he said as he moved. The bed shifted under him as he parted her legs and, kneeling between them, leaned over her, blowing softly on her back.

"Fast and amazing." Arousal coiled in her belly again.

"Now I'm gonna fuck you nice and slow, Gabriella."

Her eyes shot open as his cock, hard and needy already, rested against her butt, and everything in her pulsed from there now. With his weight over her, she shivered and angled her pussy into the bed, desperate for friction. He pulled her to him, and her nipples pebbled against the sheet as he lifted her ass and smoothed a hand between her and the bed to play with her belly, up to toy with her nipples. Finding his way over her body. Finally, as if she'd called him there, he cupped her, teased one finger then two into her wet heat. When he finally paused to roll a condom on, he notched himself slowly inside her and she clenched around him, pulling a groan from deep inside him. It thrilled her, to affect him this way and she pushed back toward him.

"Nuh-uh. Nice and slow, gorgeous." He moved his hands, smoothing them over her butt, holding her hips steady so he could pull out and sink in, torturing her with his lazy, sensual pace.

So she let him, let her head fall to the pillow, let him hold her hips up, let him drag through her folds causing her to shake with her need. She let herself feel how thick and hard he was in her, for her, while she whimpered and moaned and lost herself to the sensations.

"Fuck," he swore and quickened the pace. "Even when you let me have my way, your muscles pull me in. I can feel you squeezing me."

"Uh-huh," she moaned as he thrust in deep and used his hand to play with her clit, his front sliding along her back with each thrust. The first flutters of her orgasm made her gasp and clench. She couldn't help it — she was whimpering and returning his thrusts, wild and out of control. Until he came fully over her, tangled his hand in her hair and dragged her head to the side so he could kiss her as he rocked her world into outer space one more time.

* * * *

"I should go," she said, her eyes tired, her body exhausted in the best possible way, a melty boneless heap of after sex. Luca had used her so wonderfully. "Mm." She stretched like a cat under the sun taking a long, long nap. "You have the best bed."

He'd tossed the second condom and returned with a warm washcloth and carefully wiped her clean. Then he'd tugged her body to his as if he never intended to exit this bed again. She'd giggled and snuggled into him. It was dark, but not too late and they'd spent the last half hour, boneless, making dopy faces at each other and chatting about silly stuff, like they were twenty and in love for the first time, the whole world ahead of them.

"I want you to stay." Luca nuzzled his lips along her neck. "I want you to stay forever."

But they weren't those naïve young people anymore. *Forever*. How could he even feel that already? Or recognize it? Gabby's heart wasn't boneless anymore. It skipped again, and she gently nudged Luca away and sat up, rubbing the spot on her chest that was suddenly buzzing with nerves, with worry.

"That sounds lovely," she lied, infusing her words with a light playfulness she suddenly no longer felt. This wasn't her home, her family. This place wasn't hers to stay forever. He'd *never* want that once he discovered the truth. Would he? John hadn't. And oh, how that still stung to think about still.

"Hey." Luca dragged his boxers and T-shirt on as she dressed. "Something happened. Talk to me. You can tell me anything."

Could she? She was so afraid. It would come crashing down around her, this new budding relationship they were building and, selfish though it may be, she wasn't ready to walk away or burn it to the ground yet.

"Was that all too much too soon?"

It's not, she wanted to scream. *It's wonderful. It's everything I ever wanted, almost.* Only she couldn't give him everything he wanted because she was the flawed one. "No," she said and took his hand, trying to be as honest as she could. "This was such a great night, all of it. I don't want to confuse the girls." *Or myself.* "And I could easily fall asleep with you." It was the truth, most of it. And as he studied her, she sensed he knew that, but let it go for now, gentle man that he was.

He wrapped her up in his arms. Allowing his warmth to mask her fear, she hugged him back and held on.

Chapter Twenty

"This seat taken?"

Gabby blushed at the sound of his voice before she even looked up and witnessed how cute he was. When she did, his smile nearly blew her away. It was Tuesday evening at the weekly meeting for the festival. She'd seen him working his big sexy butt off this morning when she'd arrived at her salon. She'd changed course and gotten him a coffee, delivering it to him with a light kiss, apparently dismissing her self-protections left and right.

She'd left his house Sunday night overwhelmed by her emotions, the good and the scary ones. The confusing part was that the good emotions were also the scary ones. She wanted to sink into his open arms of dreams for them. He was so confident in what he wanted, and he said he wanted her. He said he wanted her to stay forever. *I don't know how to believe in these feelings.*

Sweet man that he was, he'd texted her that night to make sure she'd gotten home all right. They'd seen each other yesterday morning in town when he'd brought her a coffee and a precious kiss on the cheek. No questions, no heavy words, only kindness. He was patiently waiting for her to work through her emotions.

There was so much bubbling around inside her and as afraid as she was at getting caught up in another man and letting her true self be shoved aside, she was more afraid of falling for Luca Rossi and having him change his mind about her. Her true fear right there. It was so damn hard to…to know, to see the light at the end of the tunnel. It should have been too much, too soon, as he'd said, but it sure didn't feel that way in her heart, in her soul. *Scary indeed.*

"Hi," she said, incapable of offering other words.

He leaned in, gave her hand a gentle squeeze and whispered, "Probably shouldn't kiss you here, huh?"

"Uh…" *Where? On the ear, below that on my neck, which makes my entire body shiver. Should he not, though?*

"Wouldn't be appropriate, would it, in front of all these people?"

Oh, he means in public.

"Considering I might not be able to stop. Considering all the things I want to do to you," he whispered before he moved his mouth away from her ear, leaving her swooning and, like a fool, leaning toward him. A happy fool, however. Even if she was aroused in a meeting full of people and couldn't take him up on his lovely, *lovely* suggestion.

"Luca, are we going to have enough flowers for the festival?" Nina asked. "We haven't had much rain and things are blooming ahead of schedule."

"I think we'll be good, we can supplement with some whites and soft reds, if Gabby's okay with that, in regards to her theme?"

"Yeah, that...sounds good." How was she supposed to jump into this meeting and talk about flowers, when she wanted to climb onto Luca's lap and fit her body into his? When he gave a soft laugh, it floated across her skin and had her libido doing flips.

Nina moved on to ask one of the food vendors a question and Luca whispered, "Can I buy you that drink after tonight's meeting? The one I stupidly offered after offending you that first time?"

"Your offer wasn't stupid." Her cheeks heated at the memory of how cute and open he'd been and how achingly awkward she'd reacted.

The tender expression on his face at her words melted her heart even more.

"I'm glad," he answered, and they stared at each other, two lost fools.

* * * *

"So, we finally get our first date." Luca took her hand as soon as they left the meeting. "Hungry too or just drinks? I have Daisy till nine."

"Is it ridiculous to call it our first date after...well, after everything?" Gabby laughed softly and took the opportunity to walk close to him. She loved how he didn't simply hold her hand, but linked their fingers together, locking them in place. Cool spring nights had surprised them this week. Even the rain was supposed to make an appearance tonight. But his warmth was a draw no matter the weather. Every time he touched her, something furled open inside her.

"Nothing about you is ridiculous, Gabriella. I think you and I are making our own path."

I want that. Can we really have that? "Then let's go sit in a cozy booth at Donny's and eat the best greasy pepperoni pizza with cheap wine."

"Sounds awesome."

Monday night wasn't busy, and they got to pick their booth. Luca slid right in beside Gabriella, crowding her in the best way. "So tell me more about your family. It didn't seem appropriate to talk about parents the nights I've had you to myself. Plus, I had other things on my mind, but since I can't get you naked right now, let's have some fantastic conversation."

Gabby laughed that low, husky laugh, but here in the restaurant where they snuggled next to each other, he could pretend it was intended for him alone. "No, we definitely weren't doing much talking, either night, were we?"

He ran his thumb across her lips and gave her a quick kiss, almost allowing himself to sink in. "Focus, woman. No teasing out in the open when I'm restricted."

"Me." She shook her head and rolled those pretty eyes of hers, all lit up tonight, wide open. Like she'd tell him anything if he asked. If only he knew the right questions to get her to open fully. There were things she was guarding. He'd noticed flickers here and there, especially Sunday night right before she'd left. He didn't want her to feel like she couldn't be her true self with him, every last part of her. Just because he saw a lifetime with her, didn't mean she felt the same.

They ordered pizza and sipped red wine. The table had a white sheet of paper over the red checked tablecloth and Gabriella drew while she talked. "Oh, before I forget, you and the girls are invited to my dad's cookout this weekend. I'm sure they'll want to interrogate you. I…since, well, since California, they've amped up their battle gear to make sure no one will ever hurt me again."

He smiled. "I can take it." He had no intention of hurting her. He simply had to prove it.

"And…"

Her eyebrows drew together. He braced himself. *There it is, she's worried about something again.*

"He has a pool too, Luca. Maybe…"

He let out a deep breath. A pool he could handle. She rolled her bottom lip in, and he was momentarily distracted.

"Maybe…do you want to think about getting swimsuits for the girls? I know it's not my business, but…"

"It's a good idea. Will you help me? Hold my hand and don't let me cave. Baby steps?"

She melted right into his arms with a soft laugh. "Of course. Hey, um…why *are* you so afraid for them to swim? I wondered maybe if that was how their mom died because of what Tess said at Lily's pool that day, about someone drowning a long time ago."

"Oh shoot," Luca said, remembering Tess's words. His chest hurt every time he thought of the accident. "No…it was my brother, when I was a teenager, at the shore one day." Ripping it off quickly, an old band-aid, yet it still lanced across his soul.

"Oh, Luca, I'm so sorry." She tangled her arm through his and leaned in close. Her warmth, her scent, her compassion nearly brought him to his knees. "What was his name?"

No one had asked him that in a very long time. Of course, most people he met since then didn't even know he had a brother. Even Noelle never spoke about him. Cracks formed inside him, a fault line deciding to tremble after so many years dormant. She squeezed his arm, and that small gesture dislodged the stone in his throat.

"Dominic. Dom, we called him. He was twenty-one, two years older than me. He and his friends were sailing. They got caught in a storm. He fell...hit his head and went over. I never forgave him for dying." It was a truth he preferred not to acknowledge.

"It broke your heart," she whispered.

"Yeah." Talking about Dom was infinitely harder than talking about Noelle. He fucking missed his brother, still, all these years later, his best friend. And how strange that talking about the worst times in his life could make him feel so close to this beauty before him. "You want to know something seriously odd?" he asked.

"Anything," she replied.

"Tess and Emi obviously never knew my brother. And I've never once mentioned how he died. They hardly know a thing about him, except that I loved him and we were obsessed with *Star Wars* as boys."

"Wow," she said. "I've read that we carry our ancestors' traumas with us, in our DNA. Even the traumas we've never actually heard. It seems strange, and yet, not really as I get older, to imagine that being true."

He knew this woman had doubts about herself, about them and what was happening—he could see them written across her face at times, and he couldn't for the life of him understand why. She was incredible, smart and funny, bossy and vulnerable and so, so strong.

"You're right," he added. "What an absurd idea, and also I can totally understand it." He took a sip of his wine. "So we're all basically screwed for life, huh?"

She gave a soft laugh, right into his body. "I guess so."

He gave her a squeeze. "I want to hear about your family, how you're all related. I need the family tree."

"Well, Mary and Dad had me and Cammy. Then— and I don't know all the details..." She paused and gazed off, lost in her own head for a moment. "Maybe I should ask. They were young and grew up together. They've always said they fell out of love, but I don't know if they were ever in deep love with each other, not really. Not the way Mom and Isa are now and Dad and Julia."

She studied their joined hands resting on the table. "I never thought about it before. It's different when you're a child. I was sad at first when they got divorced, but honestly not that sad because I didn't really know what that meant. Isa and her son, Javier, who was a year older than me, came into our lives so soon. And Dad and Julia got married and had my sisters. I felt surrounded by more love, a different kind but still love, safe and happy. We weren't rich. We walked to school and spent time at both houses, all the kids, playing together. The kind of childhood where you play outside until dark when someone's parents call you in. I'm so lucky when I think about it."

"Yeah," Luca said, ghosting his thumb over the back of her hand, feeling the delicate veins beneath her skin, long powerful fingers, pretty sparkly tipped nails. She was all those things, delicate, powerful and pretty at the same time. And more, all the places inside he couldn't see that added together to create something precious.

"I think maybe I lost that luck for a while, lost myself..."

He brought his gaze to meet hers. Eyes still wide open, a hint of vulnerability in them now.

"I don't...I don't know if I've fully gotten that lucky part of myself back, fully found myself yet."

There she is, one petal opening to reveal part of her beating heart, her fears and insecurities.

"Losing and finding ourselves is a tough one. I understand that. But luck, I don't know. Is it something you can lose? I mean, your family obviously adores you. You've opened your dream salon. You put all this joy out around you. When you're hurt and angry you stand up for yourself. I know some days are harder than others and there are parts of you I may not see, but from my view your luck is still with you. If that's what it's really called.

"I'm not saying the way other people have treated you, or hurt you, doesn't matter. Jesus, I know it does. Maybe it's a new kind of luck, or a new you altogether. Sorry." He poured them more wine. "Got carried away thinking about my own path too, I guess. I know it doesn't matter what *I* think about you. It matters what's in here." He tapped her chest. "What *you* believe. But those are my thoughts for what they're worth."

"Wow, Luca." She brought their joined hands to her mouth and placed a kiss on his palm. Her touch was a balm to his soul that had been drifting for a long time now. "You say the most beautiful things."

"I'm a dork."

She shook her head. "Nuh-uh. Or if you are, you're a sexy, hot dork and that is a really, *really* nice combination."

"Yeah?" He grinned and leaned in to kiss her again. How could he help it? Her energy was a lure. His other hand made its way to her thigh. Warm and soft under his hand. Slowly, he inched under the fabric of her skirt to her skin.

"Yeah," she whispered against his lips as a shudder moved through her.

He ran his thumb along the smoothness he discovered there, and even though he'd felt it before, had his mouth there, breathed in her scent, it still felt like some glorious new find. Slowly he inched higher to feel her heat. Their pizza arrived, but neither one of them moved away from the other.

"Pizza's here."

The hum of her words buzzed right through him. He had to remind himself they were in a restaurant with other people all around them. Watching her the entire time, he pulled himself away, both his lips and his hand. "How hungry are you?"

"Hungry?" Her eyes were dazed as she smiled at him, their other hands still tangled together.

His phone rang, dragging him away from the brink, barely. "Daisy? Yeah. Shoot. Don't apologize. You did the right thing. I'll be right there."

"What happened?"

"Emi fell and hurt her arm. She won't stop crying and Daisy's worried it's more than a fussy tired kid."

"Oh no, Luca."

"I'm so sorry. Here." He tossed his cash on the table, leaned in, put his hand around her neck and pulled her to him. "Eat and drink and dream about what we might be doing if we hadn't gotten interrupted. I know I will."

"Do you want me to come with you? I can help."

Fuck, yes, he did, but it wasn't fair to Gabby. "If Emi's having a meltdown, it's not a pretty sight. Maybe I can indoctrinate you into that special event after you've totally fallen for me."

He tried to make light of it. Why hadn't he said yes and dragged Gabby out of there with him? He was so used to handling things on his own, but did he still have to? *What am I really afraid of, that she won't be able to handle us when we're cranky, or that she won't want to?* Two little girls were a huge responsibility. Luca's heart thudded with the questions, questions he couldn't answer.

"Okay." She was quiet, some of her light dimmed. "Call me or text me if you can. Let me know how she is."

"Yeah. And I fucking promise to get this date thing right, one of these times." He brushed his fingers along her chin one last time before he pulled away. Glancing down, he saw she'd drawn their hands linked together on the paper tablecloth with little hearts around it. He closed his eyes briefly to cement it to memory, wondering if she'd even realized what she'd drawn. And wondering if he'd made the right decision in not bringing her with him.

Chapter Twenty-One

"Hey." Luca's voice was low and soft over the phone.

"Luca, how is she? How are you?" It was after midnight, but Gabby was still up reading. Losing herself in a good historical romance novel was a perfect way to quell the worry in her gut over Luca and his girls. And, selfish or not, her *maybe* place in their lives. She'd jumped at the chance during dinner to go with him to help, and he'd said no. She'd worked extremely hard not to show the hurt that had caused her because it wasn't about her at that moment, it was about Emi. But as soon as he'd left the insecurities had rolled through her.

Was he worried about how she'd handle a child having a bad night? Did he not want to share that part of his life with her and if so did that mean he didn't want something serious with her? Had she misunderstood his signals so far? Or had she ruined things the other night by showing her fear?

Her mind had been going a mile a minute since he walked out of Donny's. She'd even ignored her friend Jake who was sitting alone at the bar. She'd brought the pizza and leftover wine home with her and put them both in her fridge, her appetite gone. Mostly she was worried about Emi. Against the voice in her head telling her not to be too pushy, she'd texted him after a couple of hours to see if everyone was okay.

Around ten she'd gotten a quick reply.

Luca: She broke her arm. We're at the ER. She's getting a cast. Guess what color?

Gabby: I'm so sorry. I'm guessing she didn't let them get away with a white cast. What can I do?

Luca: Can I let you know?

Gabby: Absolutely, anything, call anytime

She hadn't sent any emojis, because it felt too heavy, too real to be emojied.

"Well…"

Gabby heard rustling in the background through the phone.

"Both girls are crashed out in my bed, Emi with a mountain of pillows to protect her, thanks to Tessa." His voice was low, soft, tired. "Tess tucked herself in at the end of the bed so she wouldn't hurt Emi. And I'm sitting here in my tiny spot. It's amazing how much room two little girls and ten thousand pillows can take up." He chuckled, then gave a huge sigh. "And, fuck. I almost didn't believe her at first, Gabby."

"Luca." She sighed.

"She's dramatic. If you couldn't already tell."

"Yeah," she said, trying to give him what he needed, a listening ear, a shoulder.

"But the swelling and bruising. Christ, I haven't been that scared in a long time. I…I thought I was coming home to two tired girls and an overload of cranky, and I didn't want to ask you to put up with that. That wouldn't make a good date. But damn, I wish I'd taken your hand when you offered to come with me anyway."

Even though he couldn't see her, Gabby smiled and let those words squeeze her bruised and tender heart.

"In case I haven't been clear, I like you with my girls, Gabriella, and with me, all of us together."

The words draped around her, a blanket of warmth. "All of us together?" she said in a soft, careful voice.

"Yeah, it sure paints a pretty picture in my mind."

She could hear the fatigue in his quiet voice, but also the depth, the sincerity and it bowled her over. "Mine too." Gabby risked the words before she could worry a shield around them.

"Good."

She loved it when his voice took on that gruff edge, like he was barely maintaining control.

"So you'll give me another chance at taking you out, properly. I'm still imagining you in all kinds of sexy dresses. Excluding any broken arms and other disasters, I like trying to date you, Gabriella."

Gabby laughed and let the tingles spark through her. *This man.* She heard him yawn through the phone. "You've had a tough night. Why don't you try to get some sleep?"

"Yeah, I'm going to need a few minutes, maybe days to figure out my spot on the bed." He huffed out a quiet laugh.

"Need me to come tuck you in?" she teased softly, loving this mix of serious and silly they had between them.

"I'm tossing the pillows off as fast as I can."

She chuckled again. "I like you, Luca Rossi." Her heart didn't freak out when she said it.

"Good, I like you too." There was that easy quiet between them and he continued. "I'm not sure what the morning will be with Emi, but I'll call you or see you. Maybe both, if I'm lucky. Night, Gabriella."

"Night, Luca."

* * * *

He hadn't gotten to see her the next morning, and they hadn't gotten their date this week, but he did get a glimpse of her in one of her pretty sun dresses through the window of her salon on Wednesday, and when he'd brought her an iced coffee and snuck to the storeroom with her for a few stolen kisses that afternoon. Thursday evening, she'd stopped by with gifts for Emi and a meal for all of them, and Friday night her moms had invited them over for pizza, a movie and a swimsuit try-on for the girls.

Mary and Isa had grabbed a few teeny-tiny suits at the mall for him, and the girls had loved each one more than the last. God bless Gabby and her family because he was fucking exhausted. Taking care of two kids alone was tiring enough, but when one was hurt and had a cast and he couldn't do much for his own child's pain, his job felt ten times more difficult. Having help was a missing piece he didn't really know he'd been longing for all these years.

He was also aching to be alone with Gabby again. A few tastes of sweet sexy Gabriella Flores had short-circuited his brain and he suddenly couldn't get enough of her. Didn't know how he'd ever survived without her.

And now, there she was walking toward him, not in one of the dresses he'd been imagining, but damn she looked hot. Apparently, it didn't matter what the woman wore or didn't wear. Right now old jean cut-off shorts and a green tank top the color of gems graced her body. The orange straps of her swimsuit snuck around and tied at her neck. Silver sparkly sunglasses, her hair tied back in a bandana and one helluva sexy smile on her face completed the look. His gaze drew automatically down her legs, to see what color she'd painted her toes, but her feet were covered in a worn pair of sneakers, also green. *Cute as hell.*

She shocked the hell out of him when she walked right up, put her hand on his shoulder, tipped herself onto her toes and kissed him. "Hi," she whispered.

Automatically his hand went to her lower back and he tugged her in. He could hear the sounds of people laughing and talking, the splashing of water. In front of family and friends, she'd walked right up to him and claimed him.

Fuck, he was a goner. Dazed and confused and fucking in love with this gorgeous, amazing, sexy, kind woman.

"Ready for this?" she asked. She pressed her body into his, her lips ghosted over his ear, the scent of flowers and sunscreen on her skin overwhelming his senses.

"Huh?"

"Gabby, let the man go so he and his family can come inside."

Luca's gaze snapped up at the woman's voice coming from the house. He wasn't sure who it belonged to. Her sisters and Julia were hanging out of the front door.

"*Dios mío.*" Gabby face-planted into his chest, and it busted the laugh right out of him.

"I'm ready. I can handle this. Bring on the family interrogation," he said. *Am I ready?* He took a deep breath, when what he wanted to do was drag her into his car and take her far away from everyone else for a long, naked time.

"I have no doubt you can handle my family. I saw how you were with them at my opening and when you came to dinner with Mary and Isa. I trust you."

"*I trust you.*" *Christ, big words, huge.*

"Come on, you two." Cammy was there, shoving them out of the way along with Amelia, to unbuckle his giggling munchkins. "Hi, you cutie pies. I love your swimsuits! You're all sparkly. I'm Gabby's sister Cammy."

"And I'm Amelia. The rest of the fam is by the pool waiting for you." Her family enveloped his girls and finally it was the two of them, alone.

"I meant the swimming, silly man. You know, your little precious gems in the water, learning how to kick and blow bubbles. I'll be right there the entire time, 'kay? Handling them with care." Luca's grip around her softened. She was worried about his other fear, his completely irrational but real fear. But this time he was going to dive right in, literally.

"I brought my suit. Can you handle me with care too?"

"Of course. That's what I meant anyway. Baby steps, remember?"

"Yeah." Baby steps for taking his girls swimming, but not for his heart. That overgrown thumping organ had leapt right into the water in one big splashy cannonball.

* * * *

"I completely forgot about the cast," Luca said. He'd completely forgotten about a lot of things, apparently. One main thing being how to breathe and think properly around a woman he was in love with while she wore a deep orange bikini under the sunlight, water droplets sparkling across her skin.

In love with. The breath left him in a blow. *Damn.* It was scary, but when he let the thought settle, it sure felt right. Of course he would realize he'd fallen head-first into love with a woman while his daughter was about to have an epic tantrum.

"I can't go swimming?" Emi cried, mouth open, eyes full of tears.

Gabby's family was here, a bunch of cousins including José and Ana and their siblings. Jake stood next to him, hands on his hips. Luca was surrounded by familiar faces, even if he didn't know all of them well. All eyes burned into him to fix this issue for his child. Or maybe it was in his imagination. How it always felt when one or both kids were a centimeter from meltdown, and there was nothing he could do to stop it.

He'd been stressed about them swimming, although not as much as he'd expected with Gabby's constant encouragement and support. All week he'd talked himself out of his worry. Hell, he'd even been looking forward to it. He used to love it. And now his daughter had a cast past her elbow, pink to match her brand-new pink bikini.

"Oh, we can take care of that," Gabby said. "I thought of everything." She held up a big plastic bag and duct tape.

"Yep," her dad said. "This isn't our first broken arm around the pool."

"Here." Gabby sat on the chaise next to Emi. "I'm going to wrap your arm in this bag and seal it with tape so no water can touch it. Swimming might be a tiny bit awkward, but at least you'll get to go in. And" — Gabby's voice got dramatic as she continued — "you'll still be able to splash your dad." She'd wrapped and taped the casted arm while she spoke, weaving her beautiful magic around all of them.

"Whew." Jake let out a breath, echoing Luca's thoughts.

"Okay," Emi said, surprising him with how fragile his lion was at this moment, almost still on the verge of tears.

His daughter took a huge hiccuping breath and put her good arm around Gabby, and there went his heart, flopping around like a happy seal. What squeezed his emotions even tighter was the tear Gabby wiped from her own eye. Jesus, these women were going to kill him. He'd die a brilliant, beautiful death surrounded by love. What more could any man ask for?

Without saying a word, Tess gazed up at him, as if she understood the love, the weight of it all, the beauty, and as if she also understood they had no say in the matter. That they'd all fallen head-first for Gabby. Then his daughter put her tiny hand in his and led him to the water.

Chapter Twenty-Two

"I'm going to build a pool."

Gabby laughed as Luca wrapped his arms around her from behind. She'd been treading water watching his girls while Mateo and Julia helped them out of the water to get towels and lunch. He loved the laugh that trembled through her, and he loved surprising her.

"That's a pretty big baby step," she teased, grasping onto his hands and holding them tight together. "You did good today, Luca. I don't think they noticed your worry."

"You could though?" It didn't bother him one bit that his fear was visible to her. Not anymore. Every time he was vulnerable with her, she took such good care that it made it easier and easier for him to open up, to fall off the cliff for her.

She twisted her neck and smiled at him, running her hands through his hair. "Mm, I'd love to get my hands on this head of hair in my salon." She closed her eyes with a dreamy look on her face and fell back into him.

"I hate getting my hair cut."

"What?" Gabby turned in his arms. "You're kidding me?"

"Nope." He shook his head.

"Well." She huffed. "Not when I cut it you won't."

Challenge accepted. He twisted her back around. "You can do whatever you want with my hair, woman." He let himself hold her and floated them into the deep end. *You can do whatever you want with me.*

They floated in the silence for a few moments. They were the only ones still in the water. The hubbub of family laughter and eating and music toyed around them from the yard beyond. A hot tub, a grill and firepit all accompanied the pool. There was tons of grass for yard games and wild gardens trailed in a curve down a hill and into a copse of trees.

"I could only sense a tiny bit of fear, in the beginning," she said quietly. "But you loosened up and had fun with them. Could you tell how much they enjoyed it?"

"You loosen me up." If only he could beam them somewhere else, alone on a tropical vacation. Except right here was pretty damn amazing.

"Is that what you'd call yourself right now?" Sexy, soft teasing words.

"Well, not every part of me is loose, that's for sure. My body tends to do that around you if you hadn't noticed." He nipped her earlobe quickly, then kissed the spot to soothe.

"Oh, I noticed. Poor thing." She untucked herself from his arms, their fingers still linked. "Does that mean you'll have to stay in the water and cool off?" She goaded with that sing-song lure of hers. He loved this, the weightlessness of the water, the tiredness from a fun day of playing in the sun, being with her, her words brushing against him.

She started to giggle and kick away, but he twirled her right back into his arms, startled a yelp out of her and said, "Maybe. Maybe I just need to play a little first." Then he used his strength to dunk them both. She tickled her way out of his arms and escaped, laughing and splashing at him. Then like a sleek fish she slipped through the water and swam away. This day reminded his body how much he fucking loved swimming. He chased her. When he caught her, he lifted her and tossed her into the water. Then he darted away from her, but she was quick too.

Turns out playing with her in the water did nothing to alleviate how hard he was. It was nothing new around her. She stirred him with barely a glance. When she smiled, he was a goner. Touching her smooth skin while she swam and swatted at his skin was only another kind of foreplay. Damn, maybe he really would build a pool in his own yard. He could imagine it now, late nights when the girls were asleep, playing with Gabby in the water, under the stars.

They swam and chased and teased each other, until their breathing was heavy, and Emi and Tess were sitting at the edge, wrapped in towels, feet dangling in the water cheering for Gabby.

"Don't hurt her, Daddy."

"Don't splash water in her eyes."

They kicked their feet and giggled and drank from their sippy cups.

"Yes, don't hurt me, Daddy," Gabby whispered with a teasing smirk, slipped under the water and disappeared, surfacing right next to his girls.

He let her go. Treading water, with only his head above the surface he watched her smile at his daughters. She tickled their feet and elicited high-pitched giggles and cries of, "Do it again!"

Instead of swimming to her side to be next to her and probably because his girls were so close to the water and his heart still kicked in fear a bit, he stayed back and observed, let the water course around him, quiet his fears, his body, his mind. He took deep breaths and remembered all the days at the shore and at the pool as a child with his brother and friends. The smell of sunlight and chlorine, and salt. The cool caress of the water, the best kind of exhausted that came from joy.

Right now, that was what he focused on, the joy. He was surrounded by it, and for the first time in a long time, Luca relaxed and allowed the goodness to buoy him.

* * * *

It was a good thing he soaked up the bucolic feelings earlier because his girls were exactly what he'd feared he was going to encounter the other night when the babysitter had called him. Exactly what he hoped not to smack Gabby in the face with. But who was he kidding? This was his reality some moments. And his girls had played hard all day too. Now they were a few pages short of a Shakespearean tragedy waiting to happen in his arms. One crying that they didn't want to go, the other crying how they did. And honestly, he couldn't tell who was crying what.

"Can I let you go for a minute, Tess, so I can get Emi buckled in."

"I want Gabby!" Tess cried and held out her arms.

Gabby was behind him with their bags. She set them on the lawn and wrapped Tess in her arms. Gabby had put on an old, oversized sweatshirt at some point and Tess was in her sweats. His baby flopped her head right onto Gabby's shoulder and cuddled in, and the beautiful sight stopped his heart and restarted it on a brilliant new path. Soft love and cuddling. *Mine, they're all of them mine, Tess, Emi and Gabby. Ours. I want her to be ours.*

"I want Gabby too!" Emi echoed her sister as Luca buckled her in and handed her her stuffed monkey. "She's soft and I like her laugh." It came out as a pout. Damn his girls were good at pouting.

"She is soft, and I like her laugh too." He tried to grin at Gabby as he unfolded Tess from her arms, but it was probably closer to a grimace. He fit Tess into her car seat and faced Gabby.

"Want me to come with you?"

"Come home with us," he blurted at the same time.

"Yeah." She studied his eyes and gave him that tender smile he'd already claimed as his own personal gift from her. "You sure?" she whispered.

"Absolutely. I might be off my rocker asking you to come into the battle, but I want you with me, with us."

"Let me get my purse. Do you…uh…do you have a toothbrush I could borrow?"

He put his hands on her hips and pulled her flush against him. "I do." Kissing her lightly, he said, "We are very good at dental hygiene at our house."

Her grin spread wide. "I don't know what is going on, but you even make teeth brushing sound sexy."

"Mm." He could sink into her warm body right now. "It's all about the teeth." He nipped her lip. "The lips." Ended with a soft kiss before he pulled away. "All the things a mouth is capable of."

"Capable, huh?"

"Very." It was a promise and he meant it. He meant to show her again and again.

"Daddy!" Emi cried. "I want to go home."

Gabby pulled out of his arms. "I'll be right back."

"Hurry," he said.

Chapter Twenty-Three

Gabby sank in, her back against the arm of his wide comfy sectional, her legs stretched out on the cushions. Her book sat open on her lap. Rakish dukes and all were lovely, but the sound of Luca's voice from above threaded into her ears and distracted her from her story. His words were unclear, but the cadence was smooth and steady as he read goodnight stories to his girls.

After a while it was quiet. She settled into the pages of her novel, lamenting the quiet, missing his voice. He'd left the back doors open wide and the gentle breeze stretched through the screen and teased her. Most likely built in the seventies, Luca's house had some of the original features, a few good, some ridiculous, but he'd made it comfy and relaxing, even with two little girls' stuff flaked about. There was an eating area in the kitchen where the doors opened to their enormous yard, and beyond that, the sea in the distance. It was a great house for a family.

Every few pages she'd gaze out and catch the late-evening sun glint off the water and listen to the trees sway.

"So gorgeous." Luca's voice was there in the room with her now. Gabby glanced up from the page she was reading to find him standing on the bottom step. He was leaning over the railing watching her. "Sunrise, sunset, you've got them both beat."

"Hey," she said stupidly. Like they'd just run into each other at the store. As if they hadn't spent the entire day together giving each other heated eyes and lingering touches while enjoying the afternoon surrounded by family. To add to her goofiness, she gave him a little finger wave.

He didn't hold back his smile, and she loved that about him. He said he wanted her. She was working on believing him, believing in herself. She was also working up her bravery in telling him that she couldn't have kids.

"They finally fall asleep?"

He grinned. "Yep. Fought it the entire way, well, Emi did. Tess was relaxed and asleep before I finished the first book. Weekends are always harder when our routine is out of whack. Not that I'm complaining about today at all. They were also not pleased with the thought of being away from you. Can't say I blame 'em. All three of us want to keep you."

Keep you. Her throat grew thick with emotion. She wanted that, to belong here with this little family. But would they really want to keep her if they knew? Would he?

He yawned and she had a moment's disappointment. He was exhausted and why wouldn't he be? *I should go.* Before she could move or speak, he headed her way, climbed over the back of the couch and fitted himself in with her, but lower. He tugged her to him, wrapped his arms around her waist and rested his head on her belly. Catapulting her worries far away, he said, "It's my turn. Read to me, pretty please, beautiful woman."

"Well." She gave a small chuckle to cover her nerves or anticipation. There was a fine line between the two. Maybe it was both. "Since you asked nicely."

"I always ask nicely." His deep voice stroked like silk across her skin. "This okay?" He gave her a squeeze, then rubbed his thumbs along her waist.

"Mm-hm, yes," she said, trying to steady her voice, trying to be brave, also trying not to jump his bones right then and there. "It's…uh…a romance." Her voice caught on the last word.

"Awesome." He kissed her belly through the soft skin of her blouse. "Romance me, Gabriella."

"I'll have to…uh…you…I should give you a quick synopsis of what's happened so far."

He snuggled in and adjusted his weight, warm and powerful against her. "Sock it to me."

"Well, we have an eighteenth-century duke who's come to a country estate to meet with Dr. Olly Bastien, a renowned but reclusive scientist who has discovered something this duke is desperate to get his hands on."

"Desperate?" Luca inhaled along her skin.

"Mm-hm," Gabby responded, trying to mask the shiver he sent through her body. "Instead of the scientist he's expecting, there's a woman in the library of this house, standing high up on a ladder, long curly hair, peering down at him through her spectacles, demanding to know who he is and what he's doing disturbing her in her library."

Luca chuckled and said, "Ah, let me guess, she's the scientist."

"Hush." Gabby smiled even though he couldn't see her. That was what this man did to her, made her smile even when he couldn't notice. She ran her hands through his hair. Luca's entire body settled in deeper and a sound that was close to a purr escaped him.

"Poor chap. He has no idea what's about to hit him, does he?"

"No." Gabby shook her head. "I don't think either one of them does."

"Ahh, so you're telling me there are layers to this hero?" His hands were warm around her, his breath against her stomach wonderfully tantalizing.

"Mm," she replied. "All the best heroes have layers, don't they?"

"And heroines too," Luca said. He kissed her belly again, fitting his hands under the fabric of her blouse to meet the bare skin.

"Yes," she whispered, finding it difficult to breathe. The light had changed in the room—it was darker now with the sun sliding beyond the horizon and no lamps on, only the dusky evening sky. It cast him into soft shadows next to her.

Luca tightened his arms around her back as he slowly nudged her shirt higher to continue driving her to pant with his teasing kisses while she was trying to read. He moved one hand to her hip, rubbing her inner thigh in small soft circles. How could she read right now?

Luca tugged her to him. She meant to toss the book aside and let him have his way, but he took it from her and set it gently on the coffee table. *How can he be so calm, so rational?*

He trailed kisses along her skin till his lips rested right underneath her breasts, dragging in a breath, an animal recognizing his prey. Then he rose over her and unbuttoned her blouse, shoving the fabric with intent fingers. *Maybe not so calm.* She moved, seeking his touch. Giving her what she wanted, he stroked up her sides and along the underside of her bra, his eyes focused on his discovery as she lay there holding her breath.

When he dragged his thumb around one breast, over her bra, a slight gasp escaped Gabby's mouth. Her nipples were already hard and needy. His gaze locked onto hers then, his eyes the deep blue of waves racing onto shore. He held her there, caught in the swirling emotions, and her body felt him against her everywhere, even the places they weren't touching. She hummed with awareness for him. Electricity raced through the air, hot and humid swirling around them on the breeze, her breath coming hard now like she'd been running, racing toward something, *someone*. And he'd finally caught her.

"This still okay?" he whispered in the dark, hovering over her, his face cast in the last chalky blues of evening.

Gabby nodded and reveled in him checking in on her, even while she could hear the need shaking in his words. She brushed his hands away from her breasts, flicked open her bra and dragged his hands right back to her, to where he belonged.

"Beautiful." It was a snarl or a growl — something powerful anyway — that came out of him then. He held the weight of her breasts in his hands, teasing each nipple with his thumbs.

She wanted to bite those thumbs of his, those magical, magical thumbs. She felt the moment he came unglued. One deep dark meeting of their eyes, or maybe it wasn't unglued at all. Instead, every ounce of uncertainty had vanished, and he centered his intention right then and there on her.

"Come to bed with me? Let me have you, all of you."

For one split second, she hesitated as her worries clouded around her. *All of me?*

"I want you, Gabriella."

She wanted him too. She was desperate with desire. And she was ready to give him all of her. It was a good thing she was holding on. Because Luca tugged her to standing, wrapped his hands around her, slid his hands into her shorts and kissed her. Then her talented man walked them backward, connected all the way, to his bedroom, sending her pulse flipping through the air with anticipation.

Chapter Twenty-Four

The dusky blue evening bathed the room in a sensual embrace, heightening the space around Luca. He dragged her blouse and bra down and sucked in a breath. She glowed in the last stretches of sunset's deep indigo. Luca dipped his head and kissed one brown nipple, peaked and ready for him. Sucking it into his mouth, he rolled his thumb over her other, felt her body arch toward his, her whimper roll through her. And her responses were too much, he needed to feel her wrapped around him. They were too fucking far apart.

He loved it when he was kissing her, working her up like this with his hands all over her gorgeous body and she moaned down his throat. But he loved it when she cried out loud too. She was quieter here in his house, with his daughters upstairs, and he didn't want her muted. He wanted her wild expressions, her complete uninhibited moans.

"Don't hold back on me, Gabby." He ran his hand along her neck, stroking across her chest, palming each breast and those fucking hard points. She rubbed against him.

"I can't...I don't want to wake—"

Luca stole her words with his mouth, savoring her lips, lush and open for him. Then he pushed her onto the bed, dragged her shorts and panties down and climbed over her. "You won't wake them. Give it to me." Slowly, he grazed his thumb over her pussy and her already swollen lips. "You're so fucking wet. Do you know what that does to me?" He stroked and listened to her moan. "What got you wet, Gabriella?"

He pushed her thighs open with his hands, holding her there before him. Leaning in, blowing gently across her skin and she nearly came off the bed. "Was it all the teasing in the water today? Do you know how hard you got me, swimming around me in that bikini of yours?" He used his teeth against her sensitive skin, then kissed where he'd marked her.

"Luca." She panted and squirmed under him.

"Or was it the sexy pages of your romance novel? Was that it? Was it my hands under your shirt and between your legs, while you tried to stay focused? My lips on you? It was fucking hard to focus on your words with my mouth that close to your skin, my nose, the way you smell, how aroused you were." He kissed her then, at her wet core and she thrust her pelvis against his mouth. She clenched his hands.

"God," she moaned, giving it to him, giving him what he demanded. The sound rippled through her entire body to her core.

"That, right there. You are so fucking sexy, Gabriella." He kissed her again, dove his tongue in, found her clit and sucked on it while he worked his thumbs over her folds.

"Oh shit!" Her climax slammed into her, and she swore his name. "*Fuck*, Luca."

Holding her, he urged her on for more with his fingers and his kisses on her inner thighs, gentled his touch as her trembles subsided. Then he rubbed her thighs where his fingers might have left bruises. Leaning in to give reverent kisses, he felt her body flinch with each press of his lips. "I was too rough," he whispered and blew on the skin, rubbing it tenderly with his fingers.

Shaking her head, she grabbed for him. "No, no, no. That was amazing. You were perfect. I need you, Luca." Her voice was hoarse and thready, her skin flushed and smooth. He shed the rest of his clothes and climbed over her. "I need you inside me," she whispered. "I want to wrap myself around you and feel you so intimately that there's no separation. I...I..." She met his eyes, put her hand to his face and held his gaze. "I haven't been with anyone since my fiancé and all my tests after that were negative."

His cock, already stiff and hard and so fucking needy, jumped at the thought of being inside her with no barriers. He tagged one of her legs up and brought it around him, teasing his fingers along her lower back to her sexy ass and down her crease as he reveled in her breaths coming heavy and full of anticipation. "I haven't been with anyone since Noelle."

Her eyes went wide then softened. She ran her hands through his hair. Fuck, he loved that look on her face. Combined with the feel of her fingers on his scalp, while she was dewy and spent in his arms? Amazing. *This is everything right here.*

"No one?"

He kissed her first because he had to. Then he pulled away and drew his fingers over her collarbone, studying each inch of her. "Three years went by in a flash. Was either working or taking care of the girls, rushing somewhere, or calming someone. Or plain flat-out exhausted."

He sought her gaze then, all the openness she gave him in her eyes. *I wonder if she knows how deep she's let me in?* "I don't think I really saw a woman in all those years until you." Working his hands between them he leaned his mouth against hers, lined up his cock at her entrance wet and waiting for him, *made* for him. And as he slid inside her tight warmth, he whispered, "No one, until you."

He held her head as he kissed her and ground himself into her body. She whimpered into his mouth while her body arched toward his with each thrust. "More, Luca. Harder, please, let go."

Her pleas snapped his last thread of control. Her pussy gripped him and squeezed around him, so he dragged his hand over her nipples, down to her soft belly, finally to her hip, and anchoring her to him, gave her what she needed, what she begged for. For more, for him, all of him unraveling and fucking her hard and deep, their bodies slapping against each other. It was raw and out of control. His release barreled down on him as she wrapped her body around him, urging him on, but he wanted her there with him.

"How can I get you there? I need you with me, Gabby."

"I can't... I don't... You feel so good. Don't stop. Kiss me, I need your mouth, and your thumb there, find my clit, that spot you took such good care of with your mouth."

"Fuck," he swore one last time before he devoured her mouth, tangled their tongues together, and worked his hand between them so he could give her what she needed. She dragged her body against his and that was it.

He lost himself in her and came undone, growling into her, pushing into her clit when the thrill captured her once more, when her body latched onto his and exploded around him. Phenomenal.

Jesus Christ. Luca collapsed beside her, their bodies still intimately connected. He wrapped his arms around her and held on, wondering why he felt the need after everything they'd shared to make sure she didn't leap out and run again. There was nothing he could really do anyway if she got scared, except be patient, and slowly and carefully try to dig out what was buried deep inside her.

"You okay?" she asked, running her fingers down his cheek.

"Yeah. That was... Jesus, Gabby. My words are...mush."

"Yeah," she said and beamed that smile at him. She rested her head on his chest. And with the soft caress of her fingers on his skin, Luca let his body and mind relax, drifting in and out. When he stirred a few moments later, she was no longer in bed with him. For a second his gut clenched, but then he heard her in the bathroom brushing her teeth. She had a tiny T-shirt and soft pajama shorts on.

"Hey," he said.

"I think I'll be more comfortable in pajamas in case the girls come in. Is that okay?"

He flipped the covers open for her. "Whatever you want, babe."

She gave him a cheeky grin and whispered against his lips, "Babe?"

Eyes closed, body relaxed, he slipped his hand under the waist of her pajamas and squeezed her bare ass. "Sorry. Fell asleep dreaming about you. Best kind of tired. Can't form proper words."

"I like all the things you call me, Luca," she whispered into his neck.

"Good, beautiful. Glad you're here. Stay with us forever," he said before he drifted off to sleep again.

Chapter Twenty-Five

Windows down, the sun warming her face, Gabby was flying on a high of so many things as she drove to Lily's for dinner. Her salon was busy and flourishing, the hurdles were ones she welcomed because it was her business, and most of them right now were about how to hire more people because they were already busier than she'd anticipated. She liked to believe a lot of that had to do with her and the relationships she'd already made in this town growing up here, and also her talent and her warmth, the way she treated people.

It wasn't simply her own success — she was also riding the wings of Graciella in bloom, a gorgeous wildflower that had been buried under the stink of a smothering weed. Now that the weed was dead and gone, the city had been able to flourish. And flourish it was, in a charming, lovely, busy way. New businesses were opening. Old ones were making great comebacks. People wanted to visit here, to move here, to help create a beautiful, safe place to live. No longer cowed and afraid but showing off her beauty. It was so brilliant to see.

Gabby felt like the city, joyful and in love. She was having her own sort of blooming. *In love?* There really wasn't any need to question. She'd begun to fall maybe when he'd first studied her designs for the festival and complimented them so genuinely. Again, when he kissed her the first time. Or maybe it was when he said he wanted to kiss her but wanted to make sure she was ready. It could have been when he let his girls swim with her, trusting her with his gems.

She laughed as the wind blew her hair through the open window. It was every moment together. She soared higher each time she was in his presence, not losing any part of herself, but gaining so much from Luca. Each smile he aimed her way, each grip of his hand on her hips. The way she could feel his restraint, then when he let go of that restraint.

Ugh, she was a floating cloud of swooniness for one Luca Rossi. Totally one hundred percent in love with a good man. And she couldn't wait to tell him as soon as they had another special moment alone together.

She pulled up to Lily's house and made her way to the front door. She knocked as she entered. Lily had texted her to come in in case she'd fallen asleep with what she was calling her nap baby. "Hey, honey. I'm here. I brought lemon sorbet, lemon cupcakes and lemon curd. All things lemon."

"Gabby." It was Lily's voice, but it was quiet and strained.

Something's wrong.

"I'm here, honey. Where are you?"

"In here."

Gabby followed the sound of Lily's voice.

"In the bathroom."

It sounded weaker as she got closer, or...fear laced her friend's thready voice.

When she got to the bathroom, Lily was sitting on the toilet hunched over. "Hey, hey, hey, what's going on?" Gabby knelt by her friend. Carefully she held Lily's hair back and wiped the tears streaking down her face. Her pale face.

Lily gripped Gabby's hand. "I'm spotting...and...I feel sick. I need...can you take me to the doctor?"

"Absolutely, honey. Let's get you up." Gabby swung immediately into action. "Here." She fumbled through the vanity cupboard and opened a pad. "Let's use this in case. Okay."

"I'm so scared. What's happening? I'm not...shouldn't be bleeding."

"I know. Let's get you to the hospital and see what they say because I don't know and you don't know. And they're going to take care of you." She helped Lily to her car. Running back inside she grabbed Lily's purse and phone. Then she raced her friend to the Graciella hospital, as quickly and safely as she could.

"Turner," Lily whispered, holding her stomach. "I need Turner."

"I know. I'm going to get you in to a nurse or doctor. Then I'll call him for you. Okay?"

"Thank you. I'm so...I'm...my voice is wobbly. I don't want to scare him. I..."

"Don't worry about that. I'll tell him what I know and when you're able, you can talk to him."

Thank goodness the lobby wasn't busy. A nurse took Lily in right away. Gabby dragged in a deep breath, tried to calm her shaking voice, opened Lily's phone and dialed Turner. She briefly wondered if she should have waited until she had more information, but the way Turner adored Lily, Gabby had a feeling he'd want to know the minute something might be wrong, whether it actually was or not.

* * * *

It was hours before they sent Lily home, still pregnant, and doing okay. Gabby had called her moms and sworn them to secrecy, as she had no idea who Lily had told yet about her pregnancy. She drove Lily home from the hospital and climbed into bed with her, in case her friend needed her in the night.

Hours later Gabby was roused from a light fitful sleep when she heard the front door open and Turner's voice yelling, "Lily?"

"In here," Gabby said. She was putting her shoes on when Turner appeared in the doorway, bruise-like circles under his eyes, hair a mess, tie loosened, face carved in fear.

"How is she?" he asked, not even looking Gabby's way, as he tore his tie off and tenderly linked his fingers with Lily's.

"She's okay…" Gabby said as Lily roused.

"Turner?"

"I'm here." He climbed into bed beside Lily and gently wrapped his arms around her.

Gabby grabbed her stuff and was backing away, unintentionally eavesdropping on their tender moment.

"I'm here now. I've got you."

"I…I…" Lily buried her head in his chest and let out a sob that wracked her body. "I'm okay. It's okay. I'm still pregnant. You came? From Berlin?"

"Gabby called me and Hans put me on his private plane. I needed to get to you."

Gabby slipped out of the room, Lily's words traveling behind her. "I thought I was having a miscarriage. I was so scared. But I'm okay. We're okay."

"Jesus Christ. I thought my life was over. Whatever happens with…whatever happens with this baby, I can't live without you. You are my heart, my everything, Lily. You are the most important thing in my life, always."

Gabby tucked her head and tiptoed out of the house, sucking in deep breaths of air to try to stem the onslaught of tears, but it was no good. As soon as she started her car and began the drive down the hill, they broke through the dam, one by one, picking up speed. She tried to hold her breath then, to hold them in, frantically brushing tears and snot from her face while driving. Autopilot had her making the correct turns, coming to stops at red lights and eventually pulling into her driveway. Rushing up the stairs to her apartment before anyone could see her, she closed the door and stripped her clothes as she stumbled to her shower. The hot water unleashed her tears fully and her shoulders shook with her sobs.

She cried out her fear for her friend. She cried tears of relief that the pregnancy was okay. Then she cried for herself, for her heart breaking at what that might mean for her relationship with Luca. Christ, John hadn't wanted her when he discovered she couldn't have kids. What would infertility mean to a man like Luca, a man who loved his kids and family above all else? Who she suspected would want more kids so he could just keep on being the best dad ever.

Gabby had finally found a love that filled her whole heart. Another human being she connected with on every level, but because she wasn't whole, she wasn't enough for him. She would never be enough. As she sank to the floor of the shower, wrung out, exhausted, heartbroken. *I have to tell him now before I'm in too deep. Before his rejection obliterates me.* Gabby's stomach sank with the realization that she was already past the point of no return in love with Luca Rossi. And she knew without a doubt, that there was no way on earth she could withstand his rejection.

Chapter Twenty-Six

"Rossi, glad you could make it," Cruz said, opening the door for Luca. "Hey, you okay? You look like hell. Where's Gabby?"

Luca felt like hell. He felt like someone was ripping his insides from his body while he was still alive. His girls were flourishing in their new life not just at the house and the wild yard they loved, but in their preschool. They'd made friends and a found family had begun to surround them. His business showed no signs of slowing, save for maybe when winter arrived, and he'd planned on that. The nursery was hopping. And he, he should be fucking overjoyed, ecstatic and in love. Looking forward to each new day, to the laughter and connections in his new life, to Gabby and her love. He should be here at dinner tonight with her.

But for the past few days, she'd been avoiding him. Blatantly. It felt like she'd shut him completely out, left him. *Ever since she spent the night and woke up in my arms.*

"Luca, hi," Miranda called from their kitchen. Adam Brockman and his wife, Cassandra, sat at the kitchen island drinking wine. Turner and Lily were on one of the sofas, and Jake was helping Miranda cook, all of them staring at him. Dinner at Cruz and Miranda's. Everyone had gotten sitters. A special night. He knew, somehow, that she wouldn't be here, after avoiding him all week, but he'd placed one last bet that maybe, just maybe. "Is everything okay, Luca? Here, come in and sit down.

"No, it's not." He didn't have time to mince words. He was a desperate shell of a man. "Something's wrong. I can feel it. Gabby...I..." He raked his hands through his hair.

"Luca?" Lily said. "I thought things were good with you two."

"They were, they were great, until...until this week, maybe...I don't know. I saw her Tuesday morning...then radio silence. She was magically busy in the back at her own salon two days in a row when I stopped by. And she hasn't answered my phone calls."

He knew he sounded harsh. He fucking hurt. He sank into a chair and tried to ease the pain in his chest. "I got one text back from her, saying we'd talk. Something's off. I sensed something hurting her, but she wouldn't ever tell me what. I mean she told me about the asshole she dated in California, how that ended. Is that it? Does she think I'm like that? Did something else happen that I don't know about? Christ, I need your help." He leaned his elbows on his knees and rested his head in his hands.

"Did Tuesday night upset her?" Turner quietly asked Lily while brushing her hair behind her ear. Lily rested her head on Turner's shoulder.

"What happened Tuesday?" Cass asked.

Lily and Turner looked at each other before they faced the group, Lily's hand in Turner's. "Well, I'm, um, pregnant."

"What! That's great, honey!" Miranda gave Lily a hug.

"Super exciting, guys, congratulations," Adam said.

Lily studied Turner again before she continued. "On Tuesday, Gabby took me to the hospital because I thought I was having a miscarriage."

"Oh, no," Cass said.

"It's okay," Lily rushed on. "Just heavy spotting. Scared me, freaked me out. Gabby stayed with me until Turner got home."

"Why would that make her so upset she won't talk to me?" Luca asked. The others looked just as confused as he did.

"I think something else happened to her in California that we don't know about." Lily's tone was serious. "She's been so different. And it's never been like her to avoid things, but ever since she's been back, that's been her MO. It's like she shuts down or hides from us...from something...I don't know...I..."

"You're right, but I thought...she seemed better the last few weeks," Miranda said.

"Me too," Cass said. "Did we miss something?"

Nerves sank in Luca's gut. What the hell was happening? He'd missed horrible signs before when it came to people he loved. "I need to go." He shot up.

"Want us to come with you?" Cruz asked.

"No...I...I'm going to her apartment. I'll bang on Mary and Isa's door if I have to."

"Let us know if you need help," Adam said. "Whatever you need."

"I'm driving you, man." Jake stood at the door with his car keys. "Don't argue."

He might have said thank you as he rushed out, but he couldn't be sure. His mind and heart were in a frenzy of worry.

Her car was in the driveway when they arrived.

"Call me if you need anything, Luca, for you or Gabby," Jake said. "I love you both."

Luca nodded and raced up the stairs. "Gabby, it's me," he called, knocking. "Please let me in. I'm worried about you." He wasn't normally the type to enter someone's home without permission, but his past trauma reared its ugly head and all he could see was Noelle on the floor of the bathroom.

Finding the door unlocked, he pushed it open. "Gabby?" His worry was a chokehold, tamping down his breath slowly but consistently as panic settled in. "Gabby." *There she is.* "Hey." He tried to make his voice soft so as not to scare her if she was asleep, but he sounded more like a wounded cat mewing out its pain. He gripped the door jamb to her bedroom so as not to jump her and scare the life out of her.

When her eyes opened, he hunched over, put his hands on his knees and sucked in air. "Fuck," he swore, softly. It was harder to gain control than he thought, getting the breath into his lungs, forcing it out. It burned through him. A million things had flashed through his mind in the last few seconds, none of them good.

"Luca?" She raised her head and glanced around. "I fell asleep." There were books scattered around her and her colored pencils and sketchbook rested by her side. The window was open, letting the breeze float in.

"What are you doing here?" She wouldn't look at him and her voice was so low he almost couldn't hear her.

She started to gather her books and toss them on her bedside table. *Is she crying?* Something *was* wrong and she was cutting him out. She'd opened up to him this month, sharing herself, sharing her insecurities and vulnerabilities and fears and dreams. Sharing her love, even if she hadn't said the words. He wanted that back, all of it. There'd been something under the surface, giving her that ghost-like expression that she'd hid so well.

"Something's wrong." He finally caught his breath and was able to speak. "What's wrong, Gabby? Talk to me, please."

She paused. "I can't...I..." She shook her head, brought her knees to her chest and draped her arms around them, hugging herself, making herself smaller. "I don't think... I can't...be with you."

What the hell? The words stabbed through him, but it was her tone he caught onto, broken, full of despair. "That's why you've been ignoring me and avoiding me since...since when? After you spent the night? Is that it?" He wracked his brain going over the past week, for any sign of whatever the hell this was. "I mean, Jesus, if you don't want to be with me, why did you stay? Why did you say you were falling for me, for my girls? I don't understand. Help me understand. And were you going to act like nothing happened between us, nothing earth-shattering and so profound it had me believing in love again, not just love, *great love*?" He was poking at her, but Christ, he was a desperate man.

Great love. She snapped her gaze up to meet his. He couldn't mean that. He wouldn't when she told him.

And he was right, she owed him an explanation. He at least deserved to know he was worth big, enormous love, even if she couldn't be that for him for anyone. The truth of her past had steamrolled her this week. She needed to tell him, but her fear had made her cower and hide.

"Were you going to say nothing?" Pain bled from his words.

"No," she said. "I'm so sorry. I've been trying to figure out how to talk to you. I led you on and…you deserve great love, I…I…" Dammit, the tears—why so many tears? Why couldn't she fucking keep it together? "I…" She pounded her chest. "I can't be that for you."

"Why?" he demanded. "You're fucking amazing. Is it that you don't want me, us, that you don't want a commitment? Or is it me and my girls you don't want specifically?"

Each word was a slash against her skin. "No, no, no. I do. I want you." She threw her hands out at him. "All of you," she cried, shoulders shaking now with the force of her anguish. She felt the bed dip and he was by her side, draping his body next to hers in an instant.

"Fuck, Gabby, then tell me what's wrong, because I want you too. I'm fucking breaking here." He wrapped his arms around her.

She soaked in his warmth for one last time. She had to tell him. But once she did, it would truly be over and he'd pull that warmth away. His great love, his smiles, his kisses, the way he twined their fingers together. All of it would be gone in an instant. That was why she'd been avoiding him. Because she couldn't face the end. But it had come to her doorstep anyway. She clutched at his arms and pulled away enough to look him in the eye. "I...I..." His beautiful eyes, never wavering. "I can't have kids, Luca," she finally whispered.

The stormy blues didn't waver. He simply stared as if daring her to...to what...to say more. *Isn't that enough?* "Did you hear me?" She shook him gently. "I can't have kids. Your beautiful babies, Emi and Tess? I can never have beautiful babies."

He sank into her. "Jesus, Gabby. I'm so sorry." He wrapped her tighter, stretched them out on the bed together, tossed his leg over hers until she was fully enclosed in a full-body Luca Rossi hug. "I'm so sorry, babe. That's all I can say. I wish I could make it better. I'm so fucking sorry."

"Luca." She let him bury her in his embrace. "If we stay together...I can't take that from you, that option to have more kids. I..." Snot was in her way again. She reached for her tissues and blew her nose. Luca loosened his arms but didn't let her get away completely. "I didn't say anything because at first...well, I never anticipated how hard I would fall for you."

"And me you. I keep falling. Right when I think I can't fall any more or any harder, then you give me everything inside of you, the most painful part of you and there goes my heart tripping over itself to get to you even faster."

She swallowed, not believing what he was saying. "What?" she whispered.

"I'm in love with you, and I keep falling deeper. I want you, Gabby. Not dependent on whether you can have kids or not. I just want you."

"You...you're not worried I'll mess up your precious family?" she blurted. "I mean look at what you have already. How amazing they are. What if you can never have more of that?"

"Mess us up?" He rested his forehead against her chest. "You are the strength and light and joy and beauty we've been waiting for, Gabriella Flores. That's all I want, all I need. We *need* your love. You already gave it to us and there are no takebacks." His pout was pretty cute along with his precious words. When he looked up with that soft smile, she'd been so afraid to lose, he said, "And we want to shower you with ours."

"Really?" Her hand was shaking when she rested it on his cheek.

"Really."

"Okay." She was nodding and crying again. After days of trying to hold it in, hold it together, falling apart was her due. And it didn't feel so bad in his arms.

He gave her a soft kiss. "Did you want to have babies?"

It was hard to talk about still because it was all wrapped up in her past. "It was honestly not something I ever dreamed of. It hurts knowing I can't, but it wasn't a crushed dream...does that make sense? I know for some it's their dream. That makes me feel bad too, like I should be more shattered."

"No, you should feel however you want to feel."

"I was more devastated by having to tell you because of what happened in California."

"What happened, Gabby? Give it to me. I can take it. I can hold it for you."

"So..." She tried to curb her emotions at his words. "I told you I was in a relationship. It wasn't great, but it took me a while to figure that out, or accept it, accept that I let myself be treated badly. I didn't know he was cheating until after we broke up. You'd think that would have hurt the worst, but it wasn't that. I mean that sucked but. God, I'm babbling. I don't know how to tell this."

"I have all the time in the world for you, Gabriella."

"I was...I was having weird periods. I'd been having them for a long time, but I never complained because they were so short or nonexistent. I thought something was going wrong with my birth control, but it turns out I have POI. It means my ovaries don't release eggs normally, making it harder or impossible for me to get pregnant. And there really isn't any cure for it, like surgery or hormone replacement. I was so stunned when I got home the day I found out. He came to pick me up for some event. I wasn't ready and I blurted it out, still in shock probably. And he...he just sort of stared at me like I was a stranger or defective. Then he walked out."

Luca's arms squeezed around her as he growled.

"A few days later he texted me that we were finished. Said he had to keep his options open. Apparently, he already had some options on the side. Or maybe I was the side. Not too sure about that."

"Jesus. I don't know what else to say. He took one of your worst moments and made it about himself and treated you horribly and that pisses me off. I'm not him," he whispered. "I want this beautiful heart right here." He put his hand on her chest.

"I've done a lot of work in therapy, but I didn't know how much all of it affected me until I fell in love with you and realized I could never give you, give *us* babies, give you that big family you said you wanted. And I assumed the worst. I couldn't deal with you rejecting me too, for not being complete like he did. I mean, I know it sounds ridiculous in my rational mind, but my emotions were overwhelmed. I got so scared."

"Did something happen to spook you, recently I mean?" She was cradled in him, warm and loose, her emotions smoothing out. "Oh, wait, Lily," he said.

"You know?"

"I was just at Cruz and Miranda's for the dinner they invited us to. Last-ditch effort, thought you might be there."

"Oh my God, I completely forgot about it. They told you?"

"Lily told us all what happened."

"When I was waiting for her at the hospital...I called Turner and he...his wealthy partner flew him home on his plane. I stayed with her and when he got there, it...I was so happy for them, for her. She's my best friend in the world." She crumpled, all the emotions from that night swelling inside her.

"Babe, hey." Luca wiped her tears again.

"The way Turner was when he got there. He'd sprinted across the world through storms to get to her. She's the most important thing in the world to him." Gabby gripped his biceps tightly. "No matter what had happened to their baby, he so deeply loves and worships Lily. It broke something in me, something that was already cracking. I thought I wasn't worth that kind of love...with you...and not being whole, not being able to have—"

"You're worth it. You're worth everything. Do you hear me?" He tipped her head back so he could touch her lips with his, a tender kiss that spoke volumes to her. Every emotion poured into one kiss while her tears fell. The shields around her heart burned down, and she returned the kiss, trying to mimic the intensity of his feelings, trying to convey that she felt the same about him. "You're whole. And you're mine if you want to be, Gabriella."

"I do, Luca, so much. I'm falling so hard in love with you too, you and your precious girls." His eyes burned into her, so deep and beautiful. She latched onto his steady blue gaze and allowed herself to breathe and dream. "Speaking of them, where are they?"

"Ana's babysitting."

Luca. I'm so sorry."

"It's okay," he said. "I'm glad you didn't go too far, and that I could find you."

"I think I needed you to find me, Luca," she whispered.

"Yeah." He wiped one last tear off her face. "Come home with me, right now. Stay the night. I don't want to say goodbye to you, ever, but especially not now. Plus, we're kind of on a roll now."

"Oh, yeah, what's that?" She smiled the first genuine smile she'd felt capable of in days.

"So far after every festival meeting, we've had really abnormal encounters." He quirked his mouth at her. "We don't want to break our stride."

"Hmm," she said. "I really like our abnormal."

"Me too, Gabby. Me too."

Chapter Twenty-Seven

"I love your yard." Gabby leaned her back against Luca's chest. His arms were around her and he'd rested his cheek next to hers. They watched the girls play in the backyard. Both exhausted and elated, she felt sort of floaty in the soft, dry air.

"It's kind of a mess," he said.

His voice rumbled right through her. She reached back and ran her hands through his hair that was long past needing a cut, but still so sexy on him. After Ana had left, he'd changed into faded old jeans and a soft gray T-shirt with *Northeastern Huskies* on it that had also seen better days. Or, maybe not better because the used, faded look was a good one on her sexy husky.

She hadn't changed when they'd left her apartment. So she was in her comfy stay-at-home clothes, a soft old T-shirt and worn leggings with a hole in one knee, wearing the streaks from tears on her cheeks and old makeup. The girls had macaroni and cheese sauce on their shirts and seriously messy curls that Gabby might be intimidated by if she wasn't a tangled hair master.

They were all barefoot, caught in the spell of the late evening before the sun finally set and cast them in darkness. The magical hour. And tonight it was proving her right once again. The muted blue sky was highlighted on the horizon by the last shards of orange sunrays. The trees were soft against the sky's backdrop as if someone had painted them with a fluffy brush. The warm grass tickled her feet.

So many things already bloomed in his yard — a few leftover daffodils and tulips from previous owners, peonies beginning to open. Lining the end of his yard, the apple and pear trees were half in bloom, which was wonderful since the festival was next weekend. There were a million wild irises and rhododendrons fighting for space. One rhody had exploded into the size of Ohio and was currently choking its way around a gorgeous old flowering Dogwood. Overgrown lilac bushes were flush with purple and white blooms. Their perfume enveloped them in the perfect evening.

"I love this mess, being with all of you in this beautiful wild yard," she said, resting her head against him.

"Me too." His voice hummed along her neck. "Gonna have to tame some of it though if I don't want to wake up smothered in blackberry vines. And the bindweed, already racing strong this spring. Jesus, it's like kudzu."

She laughed, and it felt so good to be full of emotions and let them out as opposed to holding them in. "You could get a goat or two."

"Hush, woman." He tickled her side. "If those two hear you say that, it'll instantly become more important than pink hair."

"True." She laughed with him. "I may have a solution to the pink hair demands or any color for that matter."

"Oh?"

"I promise it's safe and requires no hair dye touching your girls' hair, at least not at this age."

"I trust you with them, Gabby. Completely."

"You do?" She turned her head to look up at him. And there were his steady eyes, as open and honest as the waves. All she had to do was pay attention.

"Absolutely. Everything you do, little and big, smooths over my fears and worries. You took them swimming even when you could see me ready to jump out of my skin not to let them near Lily's pool. And you didn't even make fun of my irrational fear."

"Not irrational, honey," she whispered.

"But I think you might have cemented my trust at the garden center that day before we went to dinner with Mary and Isa."

"What happened then?" She replayed that morning in her head. Her hackles had certainly been raised. She'd stupidly thought he'd been following her. "I was kind of snotty to you."

"Yeah. And you were sexy and cute even then. But it wasn't how you treated me. It was when the girls asked if you had a mom and went right to you. You got down on their level and welcomed them into your arms with love, no matter how you felt about me at that moment. You made them feel safe in their emotions without question. It was like you loved them already." Luca was choked up.

Gabby turned in his arms and captured his mouth with hers. "I think I did," she said when she paused in kissing him, basking in the magic around her.

"Daddy, Gabby, look! Snails! A snail hotel!" Emi shouted. Luca turned Gabby back around, so they were both facing the girls, and she was wrapped again in his arms.

"Ahhh!" Tess squealed. "And roly-polies!!" They'd turned over a bunch of old bricks the previous owners had left in the yard.

"It doesn't matter what kind, but they love animals. What do you think about getting them a puppy?"

Gabby had to pause before she could answer. Him asking her opinion on family things was monumental and she felt the pain, the beautiful pain opening in her heart at what that meant. "You're going to…" She had to start over, get her tears under control. "You're going to toss a puppy into the fray, huh?"

"Beautiful woman, *that* makes you emotional?" His arms tightened.

"That you asked my opinion, included me in a family decision."

"Yeah," he said. "Because I want you to be our family. Feels like you already are."

"Okay." It was hard for her to breathe, let alone speak.

"Yeah, okay," he answered in a husky voice that twirled through her heart and stirred her blood, sending pulses right between her legs.

She wanted to jump his bones, but she had to keep things G-rated for now.

"Can you picture it though?" he said. "A dog chasing them, getting tangled in their little legs, tongue hanging out as it tried to keep up. He'll grow into a big mutt with lots of fur and friendly eyes. Completing our family. Messy and different and beautiful."

Completing our family. She wanted to pinch herself, make herself believe this was true. *It is true.* Her heart beat out the words. A beautiful, messy, love-filled truth and it was hers and she was going to hold on and never let go.

"We only get one life and I've wasted too much of mine already. Not gonna waste another second. What do you think? You with me, Gabriella Flores? We can take it as slow as you want. Or fast, but I see us together, all four of us, maybe five if we add a puppy. I see one big great love."

"I see it too," she said, hearing the truth in his words, listening to the girls' shouts of glee, breathing in the musky lilac perfume, paying attention to everything around her.

Chapter Twenty-Eight

"It's quiet in here." Luca leaned in to kiss her.

"Yes, well…" She flirted at him with that one raised eyebrow of hers, took his hand and led him to where the sinks were. "Tonight is for my favorite client. Special. No one else is here."

"No one?"

"Just us." Gabby gently pushed him down into the chair and reclined it, slipping a soft towel under his neck to cradle it against the sink basin."

It was Thursday night, and the girls were spending the night at Mary and Isa's house. The festival was in two days, and like many projects similar to this that Luca had worked on, as they got closer, a million more tasks arose for them to conquer. Everyone had pitched in to help with his girls this week as he worked longer hours, but Gabby had insisted they take tonight to do something relaxing by themselves. Initially, he hadn't thought of getting his hair cut as relaxing, or maybe he had other naked activities in mind, but she'd lured him here with secret promises.

"You're really going to cut my hair, huh?" he asked, wiggling his eyebrows.

"You're really going to let me?"

"I'll let you do anything to me, Gabriella." Luca trailed his fingertips along her thigh as she walked by him, leaving him alone and wondering where she'd gone. Soft, sensual music came through the speakers. He could smell her sexy perfume as she neared him. He closed his eyes and let her have her way, relaxing into the chair. The water turned on and warmth hit him. She worked her fingers through his hair, wetting it. When she applied the shampoo and started massaging it into his head, he couldn't help the moan she dragged from his body. His entire body went pliant as she cared for him. "Feels so good."

"Mm," she hummed. Even with his eyes shut he could hear the smile in her voice, feel the warmth of it. "It's nice, huh, to be pampered, to have someone else take care of you?" She waved her magic wand around him as she pressed and massaged and fingered his hair, those sexy nails of hers dragging over his skin. His mind might have been relaxed and floaty, but her touch was stirring his libido as only she could. He was hard and aching for her.

She rinsed the shampoo, and the warm water added another layer to the sensations coursing through him. When she applied something else and drew it through his hair with her fingers, she said, "Conditioner." Making the word sound like a prelude to sex in her husky voice.

"Hmm." It was his turn to hum. She'd made him speechless, languid and turned on all at the same time.

She turned the water off and squeezed his hair with a towel. "Now, keep your eyes closed and stay here for a moment." Gabby placed a soft warm cloth over his eyes with some faint herbal scent steaming its way into his sinuses. *Eucalyptus.* His entire body sank further into relaxation.

"Ready to get up?"

Luca followed her to her salon chair, taking in her pretty legs, those sexy hips of hers, all her confidence spread out in front of him. He took his time, letting the image burn its way into his mind. He loved the pictures he now had of her stored inside him. He sank into her chair, and she stood behind him, getting the excess water out of his hair. Then she took her comb and slicked it through, combing it away from his face. Everything she did was foreplay.

He caught her smile in the mirror and grabbed her hand. Bringing it to his mouth he kissed her palm, breathed in her skin. "This is awesome."

"I haven't even gotten to the good part yet." She smirked and sashayed away. Of course he watched her. At her front desk, she hit a button and the automatic blinds came down over the windows.

"I know you're a magician, but I don't even know if your haircut can beat that massage you just gave me."

"Hmm." She raised that sexy attitude eyebrow of hers again as she approached. She didn't stop behind him, as he expected. Instead, she slowly climbed onto his lap, while his heart thundered and his blood heated. He gripped her thighs as she straddled him. "Who said the good part was the haircut?" She ghosted her lips across his ear as she whispered.

"Fuck, Gabby." Luca worked his hands under the fabric of her dress. "You keep undoing me. Surprising me with your sensuality and your brilliance. And these fucking dresses of yours? I'm trying not to be a fashion snob, but these are my end and my beginning. Imagining what you've got on underneath for only me to discover. Oh, fuck." Luca's hands found the bare skin of her ass, no hint of lace or fabric. "Nothing?"

Her smile was like a cat who got the cream. "Nothing," she whispered as she slowly undid the buttons that went from her chest all the way down the short dress. She spread it open, bared herself to him. Hands on her ass, he dragged her to him and kissed her breastbone, while she slipped her hands under his shirt and scraped her fingernails over his nipples.

"Fuck." He shuddered, his dick trying to climb out of his shorts to get to her. *Calm down, buddy. We're not wasting one second of this.* But Gabby wasn't in on the message as she tagged his zipper down and found her way to him with her soft, warm touch. "Fuck," he swore again. She reduced him to a swearing, aching idiot. "I need to be inside you right this fucking instant."

"I know," she whispered. "Isn't it powerful?" Her hands were fucking powerful as they stroked him, teasing the tip where he was already leaking for her. "Oh, Luca, how hard you are. All for me. Hold on to me, please," she begged.

"I'll fucking do anything for you." Luca held her hips while she raised up. She dragged his hardness through her soft slick folds, getting him nice and wet. Eyes closed, head tipped back, her hair a riot around her head and shoulders. Her scent powered around him, invaded his body, singed him with its beauty.

"I know." Her voice was breathy, dreamy, sexy as hell. "Oh, Luca," she moaned as she teased her body with his. He couldn't take another second, gripping her hand that stroked him, he guided himself to her center.

"Now it's your turn. Hold on," he demanded and thrust into her tight heat, while he tugged her hips down. Fused together now, exactly what he needed. He stilled, memorizing the feeling. The entire world on pause around them, power licked around them, her body curved in pleasure, every cell inside him aching for her. "You're pulsing around me."

"Uh-huh."

"Do you know how fucking amazing that feels?" He took her mouth before she could answer, tangled their tongues together and tasted all that she had to offer. Then he slowly drew her hips up before dragging her back onto him.

"Again." She begged for more but didn't wait for him. She used the chair's arms to lift herself up and down. Her entire body was a sensual feast for him, how she craved their connection, the way she moved, fucking him in her salon chair.

"Take it, Gabriella. Take what you want. You're so damned beautiful when you let go, when you give me all of you." Fuck, he held on to her and met each movement of hers. He was there and he wanted her with him. Luca found her clit and rubbed it. Her breath caught. And when she braced around his dick, he wrapped his arms around her, pumping into her. When she climaxed, she dragged him right along with her.

"Wow," she said. She slumped into his chest, one arm around his neck, her body languidly rubbing against his in some slow after-dance of pleasure. Jesus, she was going to have him hard again in an instant. His hands were under her dress holding her back, her skin warm and dewy. She leaned her head up and smiled at him while she ran her hands through his hair.

"Best damn haircut I've ever had," he said and kissed her even while she was laughing. This was the kind of world he'd been searching for, to find a love he could kiss while laughing.

Chapter Twenty-Nine

The day of the festival dawned overcast and a bit chilly, but Gabby had faith it would blow over in no time. Even if it stayed cloudy, there was enough color and joy about to happen to nullify all the gray skies in the world. The morning was already overflowing with brilliance for her. She'd taken the girls so Luca could help put the finishing touches on the festival and flush out any unforeseen problems.

The girls had jumped at the chance to go with Gabby in the morning and meet him at the festival later when it started. They were arguably more excited about the whole day than she was. They'd been giggling over their shared secret with Gabby all week. Emi had flat-out told Luca it was a surprise and he needed to quit asking because she wasn't sure she could keep a secret that long.

Emi couldn't really keep a secret at all, so Luca knew it had something to do with their hair, but he'd pretended to be clueless. She'd thanked him profusely in bed last night.

"One more flower, I think, please," Tess said. She sat in one of the salon chairs while Gabby worked on her crown.

"I want a gazillion more," Emi said. She was in the chair next to Tess. Daisy and Ana were helping Gabby with her booth today and they'd been an enormous help all week getting her stuff ready. In fact, lots of ladies were here helping. Her sisters, a few cousins, even Lily. Even Jake had offered to help and hadn't batted an eye when the girls donned his pink flower crown on his head.

Cass and Miranda were busy manning the Brockman Farm booth with early spring vegetables and mouthwatering breads and pastries. Lily had said she'd float between the booths to see who needed help. Of course they were all babying Lily, now that the news was out about her pregnancy, but no one was about to tell her they didn't need her help. They'd ply her with flowers and pastries, and she'd think she'd been doing them favors when really they'd be pampering her.

"Too many will make it too heavy," Gabby said. "You don't want it to fall over your eyes, do you?"

Emi stared at her and Gabby could see the little wheels turning in that active brain of hers. It was very difficult for Emi to admit when someone else was correct. Gabby could wait her out. She had stubbornness in spades. "Okay, one more like Tessa Bear."

Gabby grinned. "I think that's a great idea."

"You're awesome with them," Jake whispered. "I think they like you even more than they like me."

Gabby grinned. "It's safe to say they adore you, or at least your stuffed animal hide-and-seek mojo."

"It's about to begin," Cammy said. She was staring out of the windows at the front of the salon. People were already arriving. The main opening to the festival was in front of Gabby's salon.

"I think it's time to surprise your dad and go have a blast at the festival. What do you think, flower fairies?"

"Yes!" they cheered together.

Gabby, hand in hand with each of his girls, exited first, followed by the rest of the ladies. They all wore some form of pink clothing for the festival—even Ana in her black combat boots, black tank and black shorts had a pink scarf in her hair. All the ladies had a pink flower in their hair.

But it was the transformation of Main Street that had Gabby beaming. Her vision, he'd made it happen, brought it to life. Pink and white apple blossoms linked enormous peony blooms in runners over their heads, from one side of the street to the other. Buckets of peonies and tulips and ranunculus lined the opening to the festival and sat in front of each booth. Precious blooms twirled around the supports Luca had built into the planters. Flowers were everywhere. They even perfumed the air with their magic. It was one beautiful slice of Graciella in bloom.

Standing in the street at the entrance to the festival was Adam Brockman with his daughter, Willow, Turner and Luca with a wide grin spreading over his face. Tess and Emi wore crowns made of flowers. Each crown also had strands of sparkly colored curls that Gabby had woven into their real hair. Gabby met his gaze and winked at him.

His girls squealed and raced to him. He captured them in his arms and spun them around.

"Have you turned into pink flowers?"

"Fairies, Daddy. Pink flower fairies," Emi said.

"Gabby made lots of flower crowns for the festival, and we get to be the models," Tess said. "So everyone can see and want one."

"Anyone can get a crown, boys *and* girls. And..." Emi spoke so seriously Gabby doubted for a second whether it was really the mischief child or an imposter. "If a person wants, they can add colored hair parts to their crown. It's not for real. Don't worry, Daddy." She patted Luca on the shoulder, and he stole a quick kiss from each of them making them giggle.

"Gabby said we could have any color hair we wanted. I'm aqua." Tess beamed.

"I love it," he said. "You're both the best flower fairies I've ever seen." He stole a glance at Gabby, and she couldn't help her own smile that bloomed at the love in his eyes.

The girls scrambled to get down. "Willow gets to be first at Gabby's booth!" Emi yelled and ran to guide her new friend to Gabby's stool, calling for Tessa over her shoulder.

"I'm coming," Tess said.

Gabby met him in front of her booth and leaned in to give him a kiss. "Tess isn't whispering today."

"Yeah." He smiled against her mouth. "I noticed. You look amazing, by the way. Prettier than all the flowers here."

"Thank you," she said and pressed her hand to his cheek. "Thank you for creating my vision. It's so gorgeous and amazing, Luca. Thank you for everything."

"No. Thank you." He said it with such power, such conviction, it melted her heart into a puddle of goo. "The pink hair, how'd you do it?"

"Oh." She wiggled her eyebrows. "Simple hair extensions clipped onto the crowns. They can take them off the crowns later if they want and switch things. They could have an entire rainbow of fake hair colors if they want."

He raised his eyebrows. "Don't get too wild now," he whispered.

She laughed and pushed at his chest. "You like it when I get wild," she whispered. "What about you, Luca Rossi, going to get a flower crown?" She ran her fingers through his hair.

He took her hand and kissed it. "I do love it when you play with my hair. How often should a man like me get a haircut?"

"Thursday night was fun, huh?"

"So much more than fun, and if I keep reminiscing, the festival goers will definitely get a show they're not paying for. Love you," he whispered, giving her one more kiss before letting her go.

Families, kids, dates, neighbors and shop owners, it looked like the entire town had turned out. Any minute the mayor would give a short speech welcoming them to the first Graciella Blossom Festival in twenty years.

"I love you too, Luca Rossi." She put her hand to her heart and started backing away. "You have no idea." It felt so good to be standing here in this gorgeous town, her town, with this wonderful man and her new life, full of love. She was home. They were home together.

* * * *

Turning the corner toward the food booths and main stage, Luca stopped to watch the girls with Gabby. Briefly, he closed his eyes and memorized the moment. The sounds of people laughing and talking around him, music lighting up the night, the perfect feathery breeze on his skin, the smell of Gabby's perfume as he caught her wrist earlier and imprinted on his brain. When he opened his eyes, he found Gabby smiling at him, and that too was cemented now in this memory of a perfect spring day. He was exactly where he wanted to be, and he had everything he could ask for.

"Nice crown." Turner stood by his side.

"You too," Luca said. Turner's flower crown had white flowers and no hair extensions. Luca's was full of mostly pink blooms, thanks to Emi's insistence. But Tess had insisted on some yellow and purple too, so those flowers didn't feel left out.

Gabby, Lily, Tess and Emi were holding hands and dancing under the trees. An Avett Brothers' cover band sang on stage. The festival was almost over. The high heat of the afternoon had settled into a lovely night with no humidity, and lights twinkled over the street and the stage, adding to the sparkle.

"Lily looks good," Luca said.

Turner let out a deep sigh and rubbed his chest. "Yeah." The protective focus in his friend's eyes had gone up several notches since Lily's scare. "She's my world." Turner cleared his throat.

"Yeah." The men stood side by side, two friends watching the most important people to them. Luca didn't have to say anything. He and Turner understood each other.

"Good day," Turner said, lightening the seriousness of the conversation.

"The best," Luca agreed.

"You did an amazing job."

"Feels great to work on a project with so much fun as the result, especially for people I know."

"Hmm." Turner looked at the girls, then grinned at Luca. "Give me a minute. I bet you still haven't experienced the best part of the festival." He jogged toward Lily before Luca could ask him what he meant. Turner whispered something to Gabby who laughed at whatever he said. Then she slipped her sandals on, gave each of his girls a kiss on their cheek and sauntered his way.

"Hi," she said and took his hand, and with it his breath. How had he gotten so lucky?

"Hi." He grinned.

"Turner said I should sneak you behind a booth or two and kiss you while no one was watching." Luca busted out a laugh and wrapped his arms around her. "They promised the girls more dancing."

"Well…" He twined his fingers with hers and led them away. "Let's go find a secret spot so I can make out with you under the stars and experience this festival for all it's worth."

Gabby's laugh thrilled him and had his heart flipping over as she snuck away beside him. Yep, he had everything he could want right here in this town that was blooming around him.

Epilogue

Four months later and they were finally having their first official date, or at least a fancy date as Gabby, wearing only a sexy bra and panties while she put on makeup, had teased him earlier that afternoon.

They'd had many dates. Dinners in town and beach picnics. Date nights at home when the girls spent the night at Mary and Isa's, arguably his favorite, when he got to have Gabby all to himself for hours with no worries and no little ones peeping in or needing them. Another date night alone at her salon, where he'd surprised her with the twin antique chandeliers he'd repaired and painted a shimmery silver to hang over her pedicure stations. He'd also built a frame around the chandeliers, spilling over with paper flowers in all shades of pink.

Gabby considered every night they got to spend together, even if the girls were there, a date, and who was he to say she was wrong. The four of them were still getting to know each other as a unit and it was phenomenal.

But in general, once summer hit, their lives had been a chaotic blur of work, family dinners, late nights spent around the firepit cooking s'mores, making sure the fairies in the yard had a special place in the new flower gardens he'd planted. Doing whatever they could to coordinate schedules and be together even with all the responsibilities in their lives. It wasn't easy, but he loved the challenge. It was infinitely better than being bogged down by life.

Gabby had essentially moved in that night he'd found her in her bed and brought her home with him. Slowly her things had accumulated at his house, but they hadn't spent a night apart since. He felt whole with her, and he'd do everything he could to protect that feeling.

Luca wove his way through the gardens of the estate they were staying at, an old winery in Sonoma. He'd captured this last weekend in August to whisk her away before their busy fall was upon them. Essentially, it was an entire date weekend. He gently tugged the cuffs of his dress shirt under his suit jacket. Been a long time since he'd worn a suit, but a party and a special occasion called for it. He stopped in his tracks when he saw her across the small pond standing with her friends under a garland of vines and lights holding a glittery glass of something bubbly. He'd also coordinated the weekend away with their friends for secret purposes.

All those purposes flew out of the window when she turned his way. She wasn't wearing one of her flirty short dresses that showed off her legs, which he was so obviously hung up on, because she had phenomenal legs. In fact, she wasn't showing her legs at all. A sleek, cream, off-the-shoulder dress hugged her curves the rest of the way down, long to her toes, which were encased in high heels.

Ahh. He grinned like the fool he was for her. Her magical dress had a slit along one side from her pretty toes all the way up, up, up to her thigh, giving him a peekaboo glance at all that smooth brown skin he couldn't wait to worship.

He looked up and caught her huge smile. He smirked and raised one eyebrow, shaking his head at her. She widened her eyes at him and wiggled both of her eyebrows, and it drew the laugh out of him. This little language they had between each other with their eyebrows and expressions, no words needed sometimes. She knew what she did to him, what he was thinking as he focused on her. She liked to flirt and tease him, and it was a fucking delicious punch to the heart every time she did it, in little and big ways.

She finished her drink, set it down and strolled over to where he stood by an old Ginkgo tree, its leaves shimmering gold above them, swaying those fabulous hips of hers that he couldn't wait to have his hands on. It was a damn good thing she was the one walking because she was so beautiful, he could hardly move. When she reached him, she wrapped her warm fingers around his neck, leaned in close and kissed behind his ear. His hand went right to the slit of her dress, fingers finding the smooth skin of her bare thigh and lightly caressing as he turned her, walked her gently back against the trunk of the tree so no one else could see what his hand was doing.

"Oh." Her quiet breath hitched as his fingers moved higher, exploring her bare skin with his hand. He could tease too. "So warm," she whispered. "Love your warm touch on me, Luca. Gives me flutters every time."

"Mm." He leaned in to scent her neck and breathed in her dark perfume. One she wore on special occasions that hinted at wicked things. "Your skin is cool, here." He stroked her thigh, inched up as much as the dress would allow. "Here." His fingers toyed with the lace covering her ass, and he closed his eyes imagining her undressed, on her stomach with nothing but this lace to fuel his desire. His hand explored while his mind lusted. The lace wrapped around her leg to her center. "Fuck, not here." He rubbed his thumb over the lace, pushed it into her pussy. "Here you're all heat, dripping for me."

"Uh-huh." She wrapped her hand around his head and brought his mouth to hers. "You undo me, Luca Rossi." He pressed his body into hers so they could both feel how hard she made him. "How did I... How did we find each other?"

Slowly between their bodies, he worked his thumb against her, dipped it between the lace and her skin, found her clit. "Don't know," he whispered and tugged on her bottom lip with his teeth, felt her entire body reach toward his. "Luck, maybe. Fate. All the stars aligned. There you are." He found her clit. "Swollen and hot."

"Mm." Gabby took his mouth and gave a soft moan. They had plenty of practice being quiet, found creative ways to make each other come without much noise. He loved her loud too when there was no one else around and he could draw out her pleasure. And he loved this, kissing under a tree at night. He pushed one finger inside her and used his thumb to press while he ground his cock against her hip, the friction of their clothes adding to the intensity. Her kiss stumbled as she came, as she clenched his head to hers, pulsing in deep flashes around his fingers.

"Fuck," he swore and deepened the kiss, taking over, then soothing her with gentle lips and whispers. "So damn beautiful."

"Hi," she whispered as she opened her eyes and met his gaze. "I can't believe...I...that just happened." Her eyes were shining glimmers of light, her cheeks flushed, lips swollen. "I've never gotten so carried away I didn't care where we were before." Her hushed voice added to the magic.

"Everyone's moved on toward the dinner setup. It's only you and me," he whispered.

"Yeah." Her gaze was stunning to behold as she locked eyes with his. So focused, she poured every thought and emotion into her gaze for him. He could see so deeply into her soul. Stroking her long graceful neck, and watching her, he willed his body to calm down before he took her hand and led her to their friends.

"I need to use the restroom." She kissed his cheek and slipped through a door before they reached the dining room. He used the other one, washing his hands, giving himself a last-minute pep-talk in the mirror.

* * * *

"You okay?" he asked.

Her smile was all the answer he needed. That and how easily she took his hand again. "You waited for me."

"Wanted to walk my soulmate into the party. Plus, there's one more thing." He swept her back a few feet off the path and into the sparkly lit-up gardens. The warmth from the hot autumn day still perfumed the roses. A hint of rosemary met him too from the extensive herbs planted throughout the gardens.

"Again?" Her laugh was deep and full of life. There had been a few mornings when that was the sound he'd woken to. A few Sundays when she'd gotten up early with the girls and he'd still been sleeping. Her laugh mixed with Emi's and Tess's while they chattered and made pancakes. It beat inside him, her life, her voice.

He tugged her close and chuckled against her neck. "We should probably show up to dinner at some point. But that was fucking hot seeing you let go under the stars, trying so hard to be quiet."

"I trust you, Luca, with all of me. That's why it's so easy for me to lose control with you, because I know I'm safe in your arms."

He rested his forehead on hers. "That right there, your words, your trust, even more beautiful than when you come apart under my touch."

"Love our life together, honey," she said.

"Me too, babe. Each new day with you. Fuck, I wake up smiling, knowing the day ahead is going to start with you, or lead me to you, and end with you. Each one more beautiful than the last because you're in it, spreading your joy, letting me bask in your light, soothing my dark places."

"Luca."

"Want to love the hell out of this life with you, babe, side by side. Want to be your family. Want you to be mine, ours, Emi's and Tess's. The girls have something special for you, but I wanted our own private moment too. Spend your life with me, Gabriella Flores?" Luca took Gabby's hand and placed the ring in it.

"Oh my...Luca. It's gorgeous." She was shaking so he took the ring and held her hand.

"I want to spend my life with you. Marry me? I want to love you. Your love makes me a better man every day. I'll understand if you're unsure because of your last...your..."

"Stop." She gently touched his lips. "I love you, Luca Rossi. I trust you. And yes, I want to spend my life with you. In your eyes, I see all the beauty and strength and adventure and love in the world."

Luca slipped the ring on her finger and kissed her at the same time.

"Holy wow!" she exclaimed when he pulled his lips away and smiled at her. "Did we just get engaged?"

He cheered and lifted her off the ground, spinning her around under the stars. "Shall we go tell our friends?"

Gabby's eyes went wide, and she planted a smacking kiss on his lips. "You planned this..."

"Well, yeah—"

"No, I mean you planned it for this weekend when our friends would be here. Because you knew I'd want to share this with them. You knew..."

He gave her a tender kiss. "I hoped."

"I love you, Luca Rossi."

"Love you too, Gabriella. What do you say we go toast to our new life together?"

Want to see more from this author?
Here's a taster for you to enjoy!

My Graciella:
Harvest Moon Kisses
Sara Ohlin

Coming September 2023

Excerpt

All Vivianna had to do now was get inside. That was it. Easy, really. *You can do this, Vivianna.* Maybe if she motivated herself the way her father would, like an unforgiving general? *"You must do this."* She was here. She'd made it. Why was she frozen now? She wanted this. She *craved* this. She thought she might die if she didn't get this opportunity. And here she was. She couldn't let a little thing like the dark scare her now.

No. She shook her head. It wasn't that. The black sky overhead was full of stars, more beautiful than ominous. Was it that she'd never been by herself in her life? Was that what frightened her? She'd been surrounded by people at her father's, at her grandmother's, her assistants and servants always hovering. And yet she'd always felt completely and utterly alone.

Standing on the sidewalk, her driver waiting, watching her, and she couldn't move. He'd set her suitcases by the front door and returned to the SUV. She'd climbed out, taken two steps, let out a breath and with that it was like all her energy, all her push, all her need to get here fizzled out like someone had doused the fire with a bucket of water.

She'd fallen asleep on the way here from the airport, finally, after not sleeping well in the days leading up to her trip. No sleep, too nervous to eat, and here she was, losing her shit right before she actually made it inside the house that she'd rented for the next three months. Her very own space. Something she'd chosen. A decision she'd made all on her own.

She gripped her folders in one hand and her purse in the other and tried to take one more step. *Just one more, then one more, then one more. That's all it takes.* That had gotten her this far in her life. Softly ordering herself to take a step at a time, to ignore the hurt emotions and the loneliness and confusion, and simply move forward.

"You okay?"

Vivianna turned her head slowly. It took all the energy she had. A man stood a few feet away. *Great.* She inwardly laughed at her situation. She'd come this far to get away from the Alexandres of the world and here was another pretentious snob peacocking in a tux, his perfect brown hair slicked back, a perfect blank look on his face, a perfect model girlfriend on his arm.

Well, the woman wasn't actually on his arm. She stood closer to a limo, wearing an expensive dress. Her blonde hair, long and straight, was pulled behind her ears with a glittery but very stately headband. It was like two statues had been plucked from Vivianna's previous life and set down right beside her. *And not a genuine smile between the two strangers.*

Vivianna could feel them staring down their noses at her, the catty remarks they made in their heads while watching her. It was like she hadn't arrived somewhere new at all. This Alexandre or whoever he was slid his hands into his pockets and glanced toward the house she'd rented.

"You renting Gale House? Everything should be fine. Is something bothering you?"

"Jake, leave the woman alone. She doesn't need us scaring her. Let's go." The woman practically floated up the sidewalk in her pointy heels and entered the house next door.

Why couldn't she do what that woman had done—ignore things completely and sail into the house with perfectly poised indifference, exactly as she'd been taught to do? The moment stretched out around her as if she'd climbed onto a carousel and it had slipped into slow motion, lulling her but disorienting her at the same time, the old-timey music not keeping in tune with the swirling.

"Your tie's undone," she blurted. Perhaps he wasn't from her real life. After all, none of the men her father had paraded in front of her would have allowed themselves to be seen undone in any manner. Not a seam out of place.

He looked down at himself. "Yeah. Can only stand these things for so long." He tugged the bowtie through his collar, folded it haphazardly and stuffed it in his pocket.

"You…what…" Her mouth dropped open in shock. One didn't crumple a silk tie and shove it in a pocket. *No, no. I don't care.* Vivianna shook off the thoughts and whipped her face forward again. All she had to do was get inside. Then she could rest and regroup. She could do this, only a few more feet. "Sorry, no…nothing… Never mind. I'm good. I'm fine. Sorry to bother you."

"It's no bother. You look like you —"

"Like what?" she snapped. "Sorry, again." *Quit apologizing to this stranger. He's the one bugging you.* She squeezed her eyes shut, hoping that when she opened them, she would magically be inside the house with the rest of the world closed outside. Her sigh of disappointment exhausted her further. "I'm just… Long trip."

Her voice had risen in pitch with each word. Trying, she was trying so hard to maintain control. She slipped out of her heels and let the cool, hard sidewalk seep through her skin, then started forward again, one step. "If you don't mind. I'm quite fine."

"Right. Well, I'm Jake, your neighbor, I guess. If you need anything. I'll just… I live…there. Goodnight."

Her hands decided to betray her at that moment as she finally found the ability to walk. Papers began fluttering down around her. *Just get to the door. That's all.* She sped up her pace. It was either save her papers at this moment or make it inside and save her sanity, and she wasn't capable of both. Gripping the rest of her folders to her chest, she shuffled toward the front door.

"Here. I'm not trying to bother you. You lost some things."

He was closer now. She'd made it up the two steps, and, fumbling with the key in her hand, unlocked the door.

"I'll…uh, leave these here."

Out of the corner of her eye, she saw him set the papers down on the bench by the front door. He grabbed a stone from the front garden and gently set it on them. Then he turned and walked away.

She did her best to drag her suitcases in and lock the door behind her. Feeling as though she'd just climbed a mountain, Vivianna dropped her purse and papers and slumped down against the door till her butt met the hardwood floors. She drew her knees up and wrapped her arms around them, hugging herself. *You made it. You're here.*

After a year of planning, she'd secured herself three months of freedom. She'd made it to this small town in Oregon, away from her austere grandmother in New York, away from her father in France and her family responsibilities. It wasn't that she was brave, really. After all, her father knew where she was. He'd hired her drivers and it had nothing to do with his generosity or concern over her welfare, but rather so he could spy on her.

All the decisions, all the silent work she'd done after hours to get here, the anticipation, it bled out of her now. Slowly, fatigue set into every joint and bone. She dragged her body up, turned on the lights, and the tightness in her chest eased slightly. A few steadying breaths helped.

She was in a tiny cozy living room with a gray loveseat and matching armchairs nestled around an old fireplace that was now for appearances only. The brick had been painted white and a gorgeous wood mantel drew the eye. A series of soft round rugs graced the floors, and on a wooden coffee table sat a basket overflowing with goodies and a note. Carefully she sat on the sofa and fingered through the basket. Fresh baguettes, cinnamon rolls, fruit, potato chips, two bottles of wine, several boxes of tea and a small box of chocolates nestled inside.

A basket of comfort.

Welcome to Gale House, named after the strong wind that coils up from the sea and sings her mournful but beautiful song through the streets of Graciella, more often in the fall. An old tale handed down from a secret group of witches centuries ago who came to Graciella to hide but found their power was necessary to protect the town. Instead of hiding, they sang songs of warning, lullabies, even lamentations when people were hurting. You might hear the wind singing around the cottage at times.

We hope you enjoy your time here. There are more groceries in the kitchen to make your stay as pleasant as possible, but please call us if you need anything.

Miranda Brockman.

Vivianna had done her research on this town, its history, its charm. She'd come here to work with Adam Brockman. This rental house was owned by Turner and Lily Brockman, and here was another Brockman, the owner of a thriving café and small event business at Brockman Farms. *All these strangers living their dreams.* That was what she'd noticed as she'd narrowed her search for working horse farms willing to implement her dissertation theories. In fact, Adam had been more than willing. After one phone call, he'd asked her how soon she could get there.

All these people pursuing their own happiness. She'd been drawn to the beauty and charming history of the area, but more she'd been lured by the idea that she too might have a chance at a peaceful, lovely life doing what she wanted, even if it was only for one precious autumn.

She carried the basket into the tiny white kitchen, the only pop of color a pale iridescent aquamarine backsplash, like mermaid scales. Feeling the gnawing ache in her stomach and nearly overwhelmed by the scent of the fresh bread, Vivianna made herself some tea with the electric kettle, climbed onto one of the stools at the kitchen bar and spread the most delicious-smelling butter on the mini-baguette.

She took her time, savoring each bite, letting the tea soothe her tired soul. She ate the entire baguette, all by herself, using as much butter as she damn well pleased, and licking her fingers when she was finished. The indulgence felt wonderful. The quiet in the house felt wonderful, like she was safe to be and do exactly what she wanted, with no expectations, no rules to follow, no one to disappoint. If she hadn't been so exhausted, she would have enjoyed some of the wine and chocolate. As it was, she wasn't sure she could make it to bed without collapsing.

The bathroom mirror showed what she feared. The lanky hair of her ponytail, flat, bangs plastered to her forehead with sweat, bright red anxiety hives covering her neck and cheeks and probably her entire chest, because her body was so lovely like that, freaking out and putting it on full display for the world to see when she was nervous.

Although, she had to say, it was worse when her hives came during one of her father's balls when she was dressed in some stuffy gown her manager had picked, with her hair up in a severe bun and the eyes of all the remaining leftover ancient French nobility and who's who on her. Sometimes she wondered if they enjoyed seeing her like that. They could smell her fear, see all her weaknesses. They were like a pack of hyenas circling, waiting for her to fall.

A quick shower helped wipe the rest of the day from her skin. There was another welcome basket on the bed with lushly scented bath soaps and lotions. On the pillow rested a matching sweatshirt and sweatpants in the palest of pinks. She rubbed the fabric against her cheek. Vivianna's life had included every luxury a person could desire. *"Only the best for the Orleans,"* her father had said two million times. But right now, this fabric was the softest, most luxurious thing against her skin, like her very own cloud. She put the clothes aside, carefully plugged in her cellphone and found the white noise app she set to rain to help lull her to sleep.

When she climbed into the comfortable bed, it was like a cocoon within a cocoon, charming small house, charming bed in a charming small bedroom, all of it wrapping around her in comfort, exactly what her body had been craving for so, so long.

It was foreign at first, but her body slipped into it easily, if a bit warily. The wind swirled gently outside and sent a low whistle through the house. It didn't scare her—it sounded like enchantment and someone singing her a song.

Surrounding herself with the blankets and pillows and hugging one to her front, Vivianna tucked herself in, as she'd always done, and listened to the gale sing to her.

About the Author

Puget Sound based writer, Sara Ohlin is a mom, wannabe photographer, obsessive reader, ridiculous foodie, and the author of the contemporary romance novels, *Handling the Rancher, Salvaging Love, Seducing the Dragonfly, Igniting Love* and *Flirting with Forever.*

Sara loves creating imaginary worlds with tight-knit communities in her romance novels. She credits her mother, Mary, Nora Roberts and Rosamunde Pilcher for her love of romance.

If she's not reading or writing, you will most likely find her in the kitchen creating scrumptious meals with her kids and husband, or perhaps cooking up her next love story.

She once met a person who both "didn't read books" and wasn't "that into food" and it nearly broke her heart.

Sara loves to hear from readers. You can find her contact information, website details and author profile page at https://www.totallybound.com

Home of Erotic Romance

Sign up for our newsletter and find out about all our romance book releases, eBook sales and promotions, sneak peeks and FREE romance books!

www.ingramcontent.com/pod-product-compliance
Lightning Source LLC
Chambersburg PA
CBHW020824260626
47169CB00003B/826